Stony Brook
Farm

Stony Brook Farm

A New England Novel

Sharon Snow Sirois

LIGHTHOUSE PUBLISHING

North Haven, Connecticut

LIGHTHOUSE PUBLISHING
P.O. Box 396
North Haven, CT 06473

Illustration by Beverly Rich
Computer Graphics by Jane Lyman

All Scripture quotations are from the Holy Bible,
New International Version ©1978 by
N.Y. International Bible Society, used by permission of
Zondervan Publishing House

Library of Congress Control Number 2002111468

International Standard Book Number 0-9679052-7-3

Printed in the United States of America

*I would like to thank God for allowing me to use my
gift for Him. I'm just your average, regular girl next door
and living proof that God loves the ordinary little guy,
and wants to be active in our lives. God inspires me in
everything that I do, and I just honestly want to live my life to
bring glory to Him. After all that he has done for me,
it is the very least I can do for Him.*

*You are my hiding place; you will protect me from trouble
and surround me with songs of deliverance.*
PSALM 32:7

The Lord is near to all who call on Him.
PSALM 145:18

To the Readers

Dear Friends,

I want to thank you for all your wonderful letters. You have no idea how encouraging they are to me, my entire family and the team of people at Lighthouse Publishing. Opening fan mail is an exciting time and getting to know you all better through your letters is a privilege.

Stony Brook Farm is a quick-paced romantic comedy that I had a great time writing. The two main characters are fun-loving, spunky individuals who really enjoy the challenge of getting to know each other. There is a lot of joking and teasing that goes on in this book, yet there is a lot of serious soul-searching as well. Both characters are trying to deal with the death of their spouses, and as they do, they try to help each other along the way.

Stony Brook Farm is a story about faith, life, love, hope, laughter and second chances. It is a story about how God carries us through some of life's toughest times. It is a story about healing and how God helps us deal with pain and helps us to move on.

This was a very personal story for me to write. Reliving painful times in life is never easy and I have to admit, writing *Stony Brook Farm* put me through the wringer at times. There is so much of my life in here and my husband Peter's. I have never lost a spouse, like the main characters in this book, but I have had to deal with the deaths of many family members and close friends who all died well before their time.

I'll never forget when the cycle of funerals started. I was 19 and a sophomore in college when my dad called me to tell me that Amber had died. Amber and I grew up a mile from each other, went to the same schools K-12, and were co-captains from 7-12 grade for volleyball, basketball and softball. We were best friends. Amber lost a life-long battle with Juvenile Diabetes. Even now, as I write this, I still can't believe she's gone. I cherish the memories of her. I'll miss her forever.

Then, three years later, Peter's aunt died two days before our wedding. Six months after we were married, Peter's mom, who was like a second mom to me, had a heart attack and died at 64. She was buried on my birthday. Two weeks after mom died, Peter's brother Don died of a heart attack. He was 36. Two years after Peter's mom died, his dad died unexpectedly in his arms. A year later his sister Joyce had a heart attack and died. She was 47. Throughout the next few years, I lost two grandmothers, three uncles, cousins, seven of my close friends and one of my favorite high school teachers.

Peter and I went to over a dozen funerals our first few years of marriage. To say that it was an unbelievable time seems like such a vast understatement. The hurt and the pain were overwhelming at times, but God carried us through in a way that only He could do. Peter and I clung to each other and to the Lord. Life took on a new perspective for two young newlyweds. Life is short. Make the most of it, keep your priorities straight, and keep your focus on God.

The reason I have shared this with you all is that I want you to know that there is a way to make it through life's darkest moments. There is no valley or pit that we need to be stuck in. As someone who has been there, I can tell you from experience, that God is good and He is faithful. He is there when others aren't and He will carry you through the deepest valleys and the darkest days. There is no situation you can't get through if you place it in God's hands. You see, Peter and I are not only survivors, we are healed survivors. Turn to Him and He will heal you. Don't let the pain from the past rob you of the joy of the present. Life is wonderful, and God has filled it with so many blessing along the way. Life is truly a gift. Live it sold out for God!

Thank you again for your letters and prayers. I am incredibly humbled and honored that you've taken the time out of your busy schedules to read Stony Brook Farm. I hope you enjoy our time together.

God Bless,
Sharon Snow Sirois

I love to hear from my readers!
You can write me through Lighthouse Publishing, P.O. Box 396, North Haven, CT 06473 or email me at sharonsnowsirois@hotmail.com

God is our refuge and strength,
an ever present help in trouble.
PSALM 46:1

Acknowledgments

Lighthouse Publishing. I'd like to thank the incredible staff at Lighthouse Publishing. You form a wonderful team and are the engine behind my ideas. I dream them up, and you make them happen! Thanks from the bottom of my heart!

Editorial Staff. Patricia Stearns, William Burrill, and Faith Wegener. You have all been such a blessing in my life and saved me from many potentially embarrassing incidents. Who knew that adding or deleting one little letter could make such a difference to a word! I'm still smiling at a bunch of the typos that you found and am forever grateful to you that you found them! Thank you for all your hard work and dedication. Your support and encouragement means more to me than you'll ever know!

Beverly Rich. The illustration you painted is awesome! Every time a new painting is completed, I'm amazed. You are so gifted. You're my favorite artist. I'm you're biggest fan! Thank you!

Jane Lyman. Once again, you've done a wonderful job with the computer graphics. Your dedication to excellence shines. Thank you for all your time and patience! As always, it's a pleasure working with you! Thank you!

Dr. Brian Ference, Harvard Medical School. Thank you for coming up with the perfect disease for Ryan Jones and Ryan Smith. It was just what I was looking for. Thank you for leading me step-by-step through what HOCM is and the treatment for it. All the credit goes to you, and if there are any mistakes, they go to me!

The Snow & Sirois Families. No one could ever ask for a more enthusiastic fan club. You guys pray for me, support me, and encourage me. You listen to all the behind-the-scenes updates on past books, present books, and future books. You are all so special to me. Thanks for being there for me. I love you with all my heart.

Peter. There are no words to express how much I love you and how thankful I am to you. Your love, encouragement and support are priceless to me. You are a wonderful husband, father, and best friend. Thank you for being you. I love you with all my heart.

Jennifer, John, Robert, Michael. This book is going to let you guys in on the scoop about how mom and dad met, the amazing miracle that we ever got together, and how we both believe in love at first sight because that is exactly how it was for us! All the teasing that happens between Annie and Ryan is something that you experience first-hand between mom and dad. I pray that each of you waits on God to bring Mr. Right and Miss Right along. You don't need to go hunting for the perfect person like it's some sort of African safari. God has someone custom-designed just for you. Wait on God...but on the other hand, you're all too young and you'd better not think about any of this stuff for at least another 100 years! I love you guys!! You're the best!

This one's for you, Peter

Peter, you're the only one I could dedicate this book to. So much of our story is in here. I remember the first time I saw you. I was sixteen and you were eighteen. When our eyes connected, my heart stopped beating and my brain stopped working. I clearly remember thinking that I'm either having a heart attack or I'm falling in love. After you left and I came to my senses and I realized I wasn't having a heart attack, I knew I was in big trouble. It had to be love and I was only sixteen. I knew my mom and dad would not like this, not to mention my very protective older brother. God was good to keep us apart for the next three years. When we met again, I was nineteen and you were twenty-one. This time, we actually got to talk to one another. The sparks between us flew and we just clicked right away. During this meeting, I distinctly remember praying, "Oh, God, let him be the one!" I was completely smitten. I went home that night and announced to my parents that I had just met the man I was going to marry! They did not share my enthusiasm. I think I scared them to death. I was only nineteen and a sophomore in college. They were so afraid I was going to dump college for you. They made me promise to finish school so I overloaded my way through in three years - I was highly motivated! After we had been dating for two weeks, we were openly talking marriage. Again, I believe this scared my parents to death, but not as much as you scared them when you asked my parents for my ring size! We had been dating for about a month at that point and you failed to mention to them that you wanted to buy me a friendship ring! Of course, they were thinking engagement ring. What a little mix-up that was.

I'll never forget the day you proposed to me. You were always so romantic, and this time was no exception. When you got down on your knees and asked me to marry you, I took one look at the diamond and almost passed out. It was not one of my finer moments. I felt so bad for you. I guess I'm just not too good with surprises. Once the blackness cleared in front of my eyes, and the dizziness went away, you asked me again to marry you and this time I was conscious enough to say yes!

You had me riding on cloud nine from the beginning and seventeen years later, I'm still there. The only surprise for me about our marriage is how our love has grown. I didn't think it was possible to love you more today than I did at nineteen. I was totally head-over-heels in love with you then, and I'm even more so today.

Thank you for believing in me as an adult woman that was still carrying around the dream of a little girl. You knew I had wanted to write since I was seven. I know that a big part of the reason I am writing today is because you believed in me, supported and encouraged me. There are no words to express how thankful I am to you for that. You helped make my dream come true. I love you with all my heart.

I love you !
Sharon

One

$\mathscr{T}$he person in the shadows took a few steps closer toward her. He was still on the outer edges of the light. Annie couldn't quite make out his features clearly, but she could feel him move. It was like a presence coming toward her. He was a big man, both broad and tall, yet he moved with the grace and swiftness of a dancer. His actions were bold and confident, like he owned the dark hallway that they both were standing in. A cold chill ran up Annie's spine and she slowly turned to run.

"I heard you crying through the stage door." The voice was unexpectedly kind and carried genuine concern with it. "I was wondering if there was anything I could do to help."

As Annie self-consciously backhanded the tears away from her eyes, she cautiously turned around to face the stranger again. He had moved fully into the light now, away from the cover of darkness. When her eyes rested upon his face, her jaw swung open in shock, and a loud airy gasp escaped from her mouth.

"You don't need to be afraid of me," the man said gently, as if he were speaking to a frightened child.

All Annie could do was stare at him, openly and wide-eyed, in a numb sort of trance, like a deer caught in a set of oncoming headlights. She couldn't have been more shocked if she had actually seen a ghost. She tried to concentrate on her breathing, and force herself to take slow, deep, even breaths. It wasn't working very well and neither was her brain at the moment. She suddenly felt that she had all the intelligence, confidence and beauty of a slug. It was extremely unnerving.

The man standing in front of her was drop-dead gorgeous. He looked like a Greek god come to life. He was very athletic looking and at least six feet tall. His tanned skin looked like an artist with incredible skill had sculpted it over his high cheekbones. His light brown hair had distinguished red highlights. It had been carefully styled and was cut shorter on the sides and left longer on top. He wore a trendy stubble beard that a toothless smile now pierced.

Yet it wasn't his appearance that had Annie stalled in her tracks. The man before her, that she was inspecting so carefully, closely resembled a man she had buried six feet under two years earlier. The similarities were not only amazing, they were down right alarming. It left her mind boggled as she struggled with the confusion playing in her head. The sight of him did nothing less than chill her to her very core.

Annie forced herself to look into his eyes. Maybe the windows to his soul would provide some answers here. He had deep blue, gentle, yet steady eyes. Eyes that weren't afraid to look directly into hers. He had the type of eyes where you instantly felt that he could see down to your very heart and soul. The type of eyes, Annie thought as she examined the man carefully, that not only search for the truth, but also demand it.

Annie knew she was staring at him. She was studying his face longer than she should have, but she couldn't seem to help it. The more she looked into those deep blue eyes, the more she was simply drawn in. Like a strong current pulling her, she had little choice as to where she would go.

Annie immediately noticed the change in his eyes. They had gone from being easy going and friendly, to dark and intense. The eyes that she had been lost in a moment ago, now studied her with intentional, calculated appraisal. His pleasant smile had vanished and been replaced by a firm, hard, unwelcoming expression.

Annie knew this change in him had been because of her actions toward him. He didn't understand why she was staring at him. He probably thought she was like an untamed teenager, gawking at his appearance. She felt annoyed with herself for letting him get under her skin like this. She knew she would have to act, and act quickly.

Annie thrust her hand sociably toward the man. In a nervous voice, that sounded faster than a speeding train, she rattled off her name. "Hi. I'm Annie Smith. I'm so sorry to have disturbed you. This is incredibly embarrassing for me."

The man stared at her hand for a second before grabbing it and shaking it almost mechanically. Confusion was spread plainly across his face. It was clear that he did not know what to make of this lady before him. "I'm Ryan Jones," he mumbled out, looking at her with a puzzled expression, making no secret of the fact that he was trying his best to figure her out.

The brief contact of their hands touching caused an emotional explosion inside of Annie. She felt an instant and unexplainable attraction to this man that left her feeling bewildered and confused. Her system had gone completely haywire at his very touch, and pure instinct told her to run.

Annie closed her eyes for a moment. "How weird is this?" she thought shaking her head, as if it would somehow make her wake up from the nightmare she had been thrown into. The man that she was trying to avoid and escape from, she had run directly into. When she had seen Ryan up on stage, the resemblance he had to her late husband was so close it was unbelievable. She left the auditorium to get away from him, and now she found herself standing face to face with him. It was too much. The more she thought about it, the more off balanced she felt.

She exhaled loudly and opened her eyes slowly. Annie immediately became aware of the fact that Ryan Jones was watching her. No, she thought nervously, not just watching but really dissecting her. A wave of extreme nervousness washed over Annie so hard it almost wiped her out. As she looked up into Ryan's blue eyes, she could now see that she was not the only one that had been affected. The simple touch of their hands made him unsteady as well. Very interesting.

As he looked back at her, directly into her eyes, his casual look turned into a stare. For a moment, time stood still. The secret was out in the open. A man and a woman, on the brink of something that neither anticipated, but both understood. More than simple attraction, need, or desire, there was a connection of their hearts that neither one of them could deny.

Annie's eyes narrowed in disgust. Never before in her life had a stranger affected her so quickly and so deeply. It frightened her and annoyed her. She took a step backwards to put some much-needed space between them. Life had been tough lately. She felt over-worked, over-tired, over-stressed and over-weight. Everything was just over, Annie thought angrily, including this stupid meeting.

As she turned to go, the tone in Ryan's voice made her stop and turn around. The sudden gentleness in his voice took her off guard. His tone was full of genuine concern. She couldn't shake it.

"Do you want to talk about what's bothering you? Sometimes it helps to talk about things."

"Yeah, and sometimes it doesn't," Annie replied firmly, letting him know that her problems were not about to be thrown on the table for discussion, especially with him. As soon as he had walked into the light, he no longer became a stranger to her. He was Ryan Jones, the contemporary Christian music singer that she and her daughter had come to hear. He was a major heartthrob of teen girls and women alike. She didn't want to fall for his charming personality, which he was famous for, or fall for his sparkling blue eyes, captivating smile, his strong jaw, broad shoulders, inner strength.... The list was getting longer by the moment, and regardless of what was on the menu, Annie wasn't hungry. She didn't want to have a part of him.

Annie was not more than three steps away before his voice cut through the uncomfortable gulf of silence like an alarm. "Hey!" he said in an excited tone, snapping his fingers together victoriously, "I knew I recognized your face! Now I've placed you!"

Annie regretfully turned back toward him. She was feeling more panicked, and if possible, more embarrassed. When was this nightmare going to end?

"You're that Christian writer," Ryan's voice held all the enthusiasm of a contestant winning a TV game show. "You're the one who writes all those romantic mysteries."

Annie stiffened and smiled awkwardly. "Guilty," she responded quietly, wishing she could crawl under a rock and hide. To be caught crying in front of a famous celebrity and then gawking at him like a heartsick teenager was something that would only happen to her. She wanted to die from the embarrassment of it all.

"My wife…" Ryan went on, apparently unaware of Annie's uneasiness, "was a big fan of yours. She read all your books, several times each!"

He ended with a flashy, yet completely charming smile that caught Annie off guard and made her go weak in the knees. As she struggled with the emotional tidal wave washing over her, Ryan's story came rushing back to her.

Ryan Jones's wife, Kay, had died about two years ago from cancer. Annie looked at Ryan compassionately. "I am so sorry about your wife."

Ryan nodded seriously. "Yeah, it's been a tough road." He paused for a minute and looked away. When he looked back, there was no mistaking the struggle of emotions that Annie saw in his eyes. "But," he said, trying to gain back his enthusiasm, "she loved your books. Your characters were like friends to her."

Annie smiled warmly, feeling herself relax some. "I'm glad. God uses all kinds of avenues to reach our hearts."

"That's true," Ryan agreed thoughtfully. "Hey, are you planning a sequel to Red River?"

Annie's eyebrows flew upward as she looked at him in surprise.

He shoved his hands into his jean pockets and chewed on the corner of his lip nervously a moment before answering. Looking at her a bit shyly, he scuffed his toe against the cement floor, "I'm kind of a fan too. You see, when Kay got so sick, she couldn't read. I spent hours reading to her from the Bible and your books."

What an incredible guy, Annie thought as she studied him in a new light. Not just any guy would read romance novels to his wife, whether she was sick or not. "I'm not sure," Annie replied slowly. She was beginning to feel like she was talking to an old friend.

"Well," Ryan's blue eyes had a sparkle of excitement to them as he spoke, "I think you should. It was a great story-definitely one that you should develop and expand further."

Annie smiled and laughed lightly. "Spoken from the mouth of another writer." She knew that Ryan wrote most of his songs, even the more romantic ones that he always dedicated to his wife.

"So," he asked in a caring tone that touched Annie's heart, "are you going to tell me what you were crying about?" As he shoved his hands back into his jean pockets, he tilted his head slightly and studied her with careful consideration. Once again, Annie got the feeling that his eyes were searching her soul. It was unnerving to say the least.

"My husband was a big fan of yours," Annie blurted out quicker then she intended. "Your music just brings back a lot of memories."

Ryan nodded sympathetically. "It's hard. I know." As he put a gentle hand on Annie's shoulder, she looked up at him, and felt as though she were going to weep from all the understanding that she saw in his eyes. They had been through similar circumstances and understood each other's pain of losing a spouse. No words were necessary. They both understood the depth of suffering the valley had brought. The price they had both paid cost them dearly. Like soldiers returning from war, they carried scars with them, yet theirs were scars of the heart.

"Here we are talking about my wife's death, when I forgot that your husband recently passed away. How long has it been?"

Annie tried to smile courageously, but failed miserably. "Almost two years," she whispered softly, avoiding his tender gaze as she made it a mission to intently study the concrete floor. "You look so much like my husband that when you came out on stage, I just kind of lost it."

When Annie gained the courage, she glanced back up to meet Ryan's eyes, and to her dismay, she found them lit with humor. He was leaning casually against the wall, with his strong arms folded easily across his broad chest. His eyebrows were raised slightly, as if to clearly challenge the truth of her story. As Annie took a closer look, she saw he looked like a man trying very hard to restrain his laughter. To Annie's irritation, she realized she was not only going to be the target for his laughter, but she was the reason for it as well. Alarm slammed through Annie as it suddenly hit her that Ryan thought she was coming onto him. Her face flamed instantly, and she backed away from him clumsily.

"Wait a minute," Annie blurted out urgently, "let me show you." After rummaging through her wallet for a moment, she proudly produced a picture of her late husband and quickly thrust it at Ryan. It was her justification. Her proof.

The amusement drained from his face immediately, as if someone had pulled the plug. His mouth dropped open slightly, and Annie felt an immense amount of satisfaction knowing that Ryan now understood that he and her late husband's appearance were remarkably similar. They looked so much alike they could easily pass not only as brothers, but also as twins.

"This is incredible," Ryan said in a soft voice full of awe. "I mean," he shuddered, "to have someone look so much like me and not be me is really a strange thing."

Annie smiled victoriously. "And you thought I was coming onto you!" She couldn't contain the laughter that slipped through her smiling lips. "That's not the type of girl I am, Ryan. I realize," Annie stated in a sarcastic tone laced with humor, "that most women are drawn to you like kids are to candy. Let's get one thing straight. I am not applying to be the flavor of the month or this week's trophy."

The toothy grin on Ryan's face sent a clear message to Annie that he was too amused by her words to be the least bit offended by them. He was actually enjoying her rebuke, and it annoyed her, knocking all the humor out of her. "It wasn't meant as a compliment," Annie grumbled. Ryan's smile actually grew wider, and he let out a loud laugh. He was looking at her so audaciously, like he had every right in the world to tease her. It only fueled her already growing anger.

As Annie lifted her hand to grab her picture back, Ryan saw her hand coming and raised the picture higher, so it was just out of Annie's reach. She stared at the picture that was dangling above her head and felt her temper rise quickly. "What is with you? Give it back now. I'm not playing games here."

Once again, Annie got the feeling that her actions were only amusing him. It was extremely annoying, to say the very least. As she was about to give him another earful, he spoke in a more serious tone that caught her attention.

"Listen, can I hang onto this until after the concert? I'd like to discuss this with you, but I don't have time right now."

Annie's Irish temper began to boil. Now she was quite sure this world- famous heartthrob of a Christian singer was coming onto her. "Mr. Jones," her voice was full of warning, "as hard as it may be for you to believe, I have no interest in discussing anything with you. Just give me my picture back now."

Again to Annie's annoyance, he simply laughed. "Now you think that I'm coming onto you!" Ryan laughed again, and his eyes lit up with mischievous twinkles. "I'd just like to have a cup of coffee Annie, and talk about this." He flipped the picture slightly in his hand.

Annie stared at the picture a moment before answering him. "Mr. Jones," she said firmly, "I am not interested in going on a date…"

Ryan interrupted her. Smiling impishly, he asked in a flirting tone, "Annie, did you think that I asked you out on a date?"

Annie rolled her eyes as she could feel her face heating up to a toasty shade of neon red. How many times can I embarrass myself in front of this man, Annie asked herself silently? Once again, she got that all too familiar feeling of wanting to crawl under a rock. "Please," she begged in a helpless voice, that sounded like a defeated child, "could I just have the picture back?"

Just then, the side door to the stage opened, and an older man stuck his head out. "Five minutes to concert time, Ryan."

Ryan nodded to the man while sticking Annie's picture in his jean shirt pocket. "Listen, meet me at the bus after the concert. I'll tell Gil, my driver, to expect you. I don't have time to explain right now, but we really do need to talk." Then Ryan made a dash for the stage door and was gone.

Annie stared at the stage door numbly. What had just happened she thought in a muddled confusion? Ryan Jones had taken her favorite picture of her late husband, and disappeared with it. Angrily, Annie paced the darkened hallway as she thought of what to do next.

"And now," Annie complained angrily, "the only way I can get my picture back is to meet this Romeo at his touring bus!" Annie threw a hand furiously in the air. "How incredibly arrogant! What nerve! How completely presumptuous of him."

As she paced for another ten minutes, deciding how much she disliked Ryan Jones and his music, a thought popped into her head. "Amy and Jimmy..." she murmured as she snapped her fingers. Annie stopped pacing for a moment. Her daughter Amy, and her friend from school Jimmy had dragged Annie to this concert, and Annie thought squinting her eyes menacingly, completely against her wishes. Eighteen-year-old Amy kept telling her that she was working too hard and she needed to take a break.

"Fine," Annie muttered determinedly, "they will help me get my picture back and protect me from this Romeo."

As Annie marched back into the Rhode Island concert hall, to find Amy and Jimmy, she promised herself that she would throw all of Ryan Jones's tapes and CD's away as soon as she got home. She never wanted to listen to his music again. She also knew that if he thought this little prank of his was meant to entice her, he had failed miserably. Mr. Jones had messed with the wrong woman, and he was just about to find out what a tornado her Irish temper could create if given the right opportunity. Annie paused for a second; this was definitely an opportunity, and she already felt her temper rising to the occasion.

Two

"*H*e what?" Amy asked breathlessly chasing after her Mom. Annie had targeted the singer's tour bus, and was moving toward it with the speed and determination of a launched missile.

"Hey," Jimmy hummed in a smooth voice, as he jogged along side of the mother/daughter swat team, "that's a good move." Jimmy smirked impishly at Amy, "I'll have to remember that one." Amy and Annie shot Jimmy a disapproving, cold, hard stare that could have melted steel itself. "Yeah, well, maybe not," he mumbled awkwardly. "It was just an idea, ya know." Amy's eyes narrowed, and before she could say anything, Jimmy held both hands up toward her in defense. "OK. It was a really, really stupid idea, and not really much of an idea at all, more like a lazy thought bouncing around inside my empty head."

Annie turned and glared at him sternly. "For future reference, it might be wise of you not to voice every single thought that goes through your head."

"Yeah, Jimmy," Amy giggled, "especially the really, really stupid thoughts. Those tend to get you in big trouble."

Jimmy just smiled at Amy as they headed for the bus. He knew he still had a long way to go before he understood anything about women. The line between getting in trouble with them and pleasing them seemed too difficult for him to distinguish at times. He knew he had to be careful or they would be all over him like a bunch of angry bees. They were a mystery that he knew he wasn't quite ready to solve.

Once they were out in the parking lot, Amy and Jimmy openly admired the maroon, silver and black touring bus, while Annie burned a path angrily in front of it. She was so mad that the steam was blowing out of her ears.

"How utterly arrogant can he be?" Annie continued her war of words under her breath. "Ryan Jones is nothing more than a conceited, vain, egotistical, pig- headed jerk, who's over-confidence leads him to believe that he is some high and mighty, self-important individual, that is entirely above the laws of the common man." Annie paused and glanced at the bus for a moment, and then went back to her pacing. "Pig headed idiot…man!"

This was something that her Ryan never would have done. Suddenly, she stopped her power pacing. An incident popped into her mind that her late husband had done while they were newly dating. Annie couldn't help but smile to herself as she remembered how her husband, who was her boyfriend at the time, had stolen her car keys and refused to give them back until Annie agreed to go on another date with him.

Her smile vanished quickly as she thought of Ryan Jones. "If he thinks this prank is going to impress me, he'd better think again. Practical jokes that were funny at twenty lose so much of their humor by forty that they're just downright inconvenient and annoying. "How completely juvenile!" Annie continued to grumble hotly under her breath. "And now, I have to stand here, in front of this big, stupid tour bus, like I've got nothing better to do, and just wait and wait."

Furiously, Annie began power pacing again. She felt someone watching her and quickly glanced toward the bus. The driver slid open his small side window and waved her over. "Mrs. Smith, I think you're being a little hard on Ryan."

Annie glared at him suspiciously. He was a member of Ryan Jones's team; of course he would say that. He was getting paid to say stuff like that. Annie's eyes narrowed at the bus driver. He had probably been given a script of what to say in times like this. Rule number one, Annie thought staring the driver down, never, ever trust the enemy. And, since the driver was in enemy camp, she didn't trust him.

The bus driver, who introduced himself as Gil, continued talking to Annie in an easy, laid back tone of voice, as if they were good friends. "Ryan Jones isn't the flirting gigolo you make him out to be. Never, in all the years I've driven for him, has he ever invited a lady back to the bus. I'm sure his intentions are pure and Christian-like.

"They are!" came a voice from behind Annie. Ryan was making a swift exit from the auditorium and racing toward the bus. "Quickly," Ryan urged, "come on board the bus before the fans get out. Gil has to get the bus out of the parking lot before the fans go crazy." Ryan turned and spotted Amy and Jimmy. He eyed them suspiciously, as if they were groupies.

"This is my daughter Amy and her friend Jimmy."

"Well, come on board," Ryan climbed up on the bus. "It's time to roll."

To Annie's surprise, Amy and Jimmy followed Ryan aboard the bus like a couple of lost sheep. In disgust, Annie went to pull them off, but to her horror, as soon as she stepped aboard the bus, Gil shut the door, and began to steer the bus quickly out of the parking lot. Annie watched Ryan disappear down the aisle of the bus giving Amy and Jimmy the 50-cent tour. Annie's face registered nothing short of fear and all out panic at being trapped aboard the singer's tour bus.

Gil noticed her anxiety and immediately set out to put her at ease. "Don't worry, Mrs. Smith, this is always our post concert plan. We have to get out of the parking lot before the fans trash our bus. I'll bring you back here later. I promise."

Annie's thoughts were interrupted by Amy's voice. Excitedly she was yelling at her. "Mom! You have got to come back here! This is way too cool!"

Reluctantly, Annie made her way through the well-decorated bus, shaking her head in disgust, while muttering the words, "way too cool". She did have to admit to herself that the bus looked very much like a home on wheels. She walked through a kitchen, bathroom area, and finally into a living room. Ryan was sitting comfortably on the large tan couch, while Amy and Jimmy were occupying the matching love seat. Annie looked longingly at the love seat, which she quickly realized was already too crowded to hold her, and then at the sofa with Ryan sitting on it.

Ryan's eyes sharpened at the sight of Annie, and he felt every ounce of himself become very alert and aware. Even though Annie was captive aboard his bus, she held her own ground steadily. She possessed an inner strength that shone strongly in her bright eyes, that Ryan guessed was only a glimpse of the power inside her. Her eyes held intellect, strength, determination and just the slightest trace of fear. He found himself admiring her even more when he saw the fear. Here she was, standing firm, despite all the odds. He knew she was not one to be toyed with. She was a powerful combination, with just enough force to pack a solid punch.

Ryan pointed to the empty seat on the couch next to him, and said pleasantly, "Annie, make yourself at home."

Annie's eyes narrowed. Her hands clenched and balled into fists at the very sight of Ryan Jones. She fought for control to keep her fists at her side, and not plant them in the center of his pretty boy, celebrity, handsome face. Instead, while she was still in control of her feelings, she sank to the floor, and sat rigidly on the tan carpeting, directly where she had been standing.

"I'm fine here." She eyed Ryan coolly, as she wondered just how long she would have to endure the bus ride with him.

An unexpected voice from behind her made her almost jump out of her skin. "He doesn't bite!" The humorous voice belonged to a tall, handsome, teenage boy, that resembled Ryan so much, that Annie instantly knew he must be his son.

"Annie, Amy, and Jimmy...I'd like you to meet my son David." Ryan's face beamed with love and pride as the boy took a seat next to him.

David stared at Annie for a second, before loudly proclaiming, "Gee, you're Annie Smith!"

Annie nodded politely and smiled.

"My mom loved your books."

"Thank you," Annie ground out quietly, between clenched teeth. She had to remind herself that she was not mad at the son, but the stupid father. Even so, Annie found it a great challenge to be even remotely pleasant under the circumstances.

David studied Annie a moment more. Turning to his father, he asked in an amused voice, "Dad, she looks scared. What did you do to her?"

Before Annie could hold back, the angry words flew out of her mouth. "He stole a picture of mine and kidnapped me against my will!"

"Kidnapping is usually against one's will, Annie," David quietly pointed out.

Laughing lightly, he turned to his father again. "Dad, what picture did you steal from Mom's favorite author?"

Ryan took Annie's picture out of his jean shirt pocket and slowly handed it to his son. David glanced at it quickly and then teasingly said, "Dad, a picture of yourself? The fans are supposed to keep these."

"It's not me." Ryan's voice had suddenly grown quiet and serious.

A puzzled expression spread across David's face and he looked down at the picture again. He studied it intently for a moment, before his mouth swung open in shock. In a voice that was barely audible, David asked, "It's him Dad. Isn't it?"

Ryan exhaled loudly as he took the picture back from his son. "Well, David," his voice sounded tired, "that's what I intend to find out. That's why I invited Annie aboard the bus. When she refused," Ryan smirked like a naughty child, "I simply stole her picture, in hope that she would follow."

Annie glared at Ryan menacingly. If looks could kill, he'd be six feet under by now.

"Before you murder me, let me tell you why I kidnapped you."

Annie continued to stare at Ryan evenly. She knew that she was "gifted" as her late husband used to say. She could stare down people with the best of them. And, right now, she was giving Ryan Jones both loaded barrels.

Ryan sighed loudly and all the humor drained out of his face. He focused in on Annie, as if she were the only person on the bus. When he began to speak, his voice was thoughtful and intent. The time for joking was clearly over.

"I'd like to ask you a few questions about your husband, Annie."

"Why?" She asked sharply. "Tell me why I should answer any of your questions?"

Ryan sighed again and Annie felt a little sorry for her cold reply. "I'm going to tell you something in confidence. I'd appreciate it if it went no further than this bus."

Annie was taken off guard by Ryan's serious, urgent manner but she managed to nod her head slightly. She hadn't expected him to start divulging secrets. She found herself more than a little curious as to what he was going to say.

"Not many people know this," Ryan began slowly, holding Annie's eyes urgently with his own, "but I was adopted."

Annie felt as though someone had knocked the air right out of her. Immediately she knew why Ryan had taken the picture and kidnapped her aboard his bus. The Ice Princess routine that she had assumed, melted away, and she crept a little closer to Ryan. Patiently, she waited for him to continue.

"I hired a pirate investigator some years back, in hopes of finding my birth parents." Ryan paused and ran a hand through his thick brown hair. His blue eyes were troubled and his thoughts appeared distant as he went on. "The investigator located my parents, well," Ryan tossed a hand into the hair, "actually just my mother. We never were able to locate my father."

He appeared as though he were trying to regroup. "My mother had been dead for five years by the time we figured out who she was. But," he waved a hand toward Annie, "we found a new twist to the story. The investigator found out that I was a twin!" Ryan looked at the floor for a moment, and then looked back up at Annie. He smiled warmly as his eyes reflected the hope he felt inside. "I was so excited to discover that I had a brother out there somewhere! Someone who was my own flesh and blood, someone," Ryan added excitedly, "who I was actually related to." Ryan's gaze dropped to the floor and he studied his shoes for a moment. As he turned his gaze back toward Annie's, his voice dropped to a whisper and his tone was filled with wonder and childlike awe. "It seemed too much to hope for."

Annie felt torn between excitement and tears. She couldn't contain her growing anticipation any longer. "My husband was adopted! He had been looking for his family all his adult life. Six months before he died, our private investigator located his mother. She had passed away five years ago as well."

Ryan looked at Annie as though he might explode. Expectation and hope blanketed his urgent face. "Where did he locate his mother?"

"In Virginia," Annie replied slowly, as a strange feeling of skepticism crept up on her. How could she be sure whether Ryan was genuine or a fraud? Would she ever really know? How much could she pack away as coincidence, and how much should she take to heart as the truth? Annie shook her head slightly. It was all mind-boggling. Why would someone fake this? In this case, it wouldn't make sense. Ryan was rich and famous, and they were not. He couldn't be after their family fortune because there was none.

Ryan interrupted the confusing running dialogue that was playing around in her head. "In Redmond?" Ryan asked, leaning forward with expectancy. "Was his birth mother located in Redmond, Virginia?"

Annie's mouth dropped open and she stared at Ryan in disbelief. Too many of the pieces were coming together to be purely coincidental. Could this well-known, handsome Christian singer actually be her late husband's brother? She and her husband had commented several times on Ryan Jones similar appearance to his. Yet, they didn't think, even for a second, that this famous performer was related to them. How could he be? He was famous….

Ryan's intense blue eyes were studying Annie closely. She could tell that he was trying to make sense of it all too. A lot was happening quickly. Too quickly.

"Ryan," Annie asked leaning slightly toward him, "when is your birthday?" She felt like she was on pins and needles.

"October 21, 1960," Ryan answered immediately.

Amy gasped loudly. "Mom!" she shouted, "That was Dad's birthday!"

Annie could feel the sting of tears welling up in her eyes. In a choked up voice, she asked one more question. "Ryan, what was your birth mother's name?"

"Alice Betts," Ryan answered slowly, as if he were trying to absorb everything that was happening. "She died in 1997 from …."

"A heart attack," Annie blurted out.

Ryan and Annie stared at each other several seconds before moving. Time came to an abrupt halt as the final pieces of the puzzle fell into place. The doubts were replaced by a bombardment of questions instantly filling up Annie's mind. She opened her mouth to speak, but no words came out. As she shut her mouth, slowly shaking her head, she felt like a fish out of water. Once again, she opened her mouth to try to communicate what was going on inside her head.

"You're my brother-in-law?" Annie asked pinning Ryan down with questioning eyes. "We're related?" The confusion of the past few minutes hung heavy in Annie's mind.

Ryan got up slowly. He nodded, and then a huge smile spread across his face. "Yeah, I'm your brother-in-law, and that definitely makes us related." He took Annie's hand and pulled her to her feet. "Welcome to the family, Annie," he said sincerely, as he wrapped her in a big bear hug.

They held each other for several minutes sobbing quietly. No words could ever come close to describing the range of emotions surging through both their hearts. Family. Finality. The long search had come to a close and on the other side of the line was family. It was better than any dream Annie had ever had.

When their embrace ended, Ryan took Annie's hand affectionately. "So," he smiled at her tenderly, "you're my sister in law."

Annie smiled at him through tearful eyes. She felt too choked up to speak, but the love shone brightly from her heart through her eyes.

"David, I'd like to introduce you to your Aunt Annie." David and Annie hugged quickly and then Ryan took Annie's hand again for a second to get her attention. "Annie, I want you to tell me everything you possibly can about my brother."

Annie nodded and smiled up at Ryan. A great mystery in her life had been solved and she looked at Ryan Jones feeling overwhelmed and awed. She wished with all her heart that her husband had been here to meet his brother. It was a strange sort of reunion without him.

As Ryan sat back down on the couch, he excitedly asked Annie what his brother's name was.

"Ryan," Annie answered with a straight face. This was too funny for words Annie thought as she tried to hold in her humor. When would the similarities stop popping up?

"Yes?" Ryan asked, looking at Annie a bit confused.

"Your brother's name was Ryan." Annie giggled loudly this time.

Ryan Jones's face first measured shock that quickly faded into amusement. "You're kidding. Right?"

"No," Annie laughed again as she shook her head. "His name was Ryan Patrick Smith. Oh," Annie asked suddenly, "what is your middle name?"

Both Ryan and David burst out laughing. "Patrick," they said in unison.

"Tell me that you're teasing," Annie groaned in disbelief.

Ryan and David both laughed again. "No, I'm not teasing you Annie. My legal name is Ryan Patrick Jones," he stated truthfully, but with that unmistakable twinkle in his eye that Annie was coming to anticipate and love. "And now I find out that my twin's name is Ryan Patrick Smith." Ryan laughed loudly this time and the pleasant sound echoed off the walls of the bus. "What are the chances of that? Jones and Smith…."Ryan shook his head slowly as gentle laughter continued to escape from his mouth. "No one," he glanced mischievously at Annie, "is ever going to believe this!"

Three

$\mathcal{A}$s the bus rolled on, the Smith and Jones family had their first family reunion. There was so much to catch up on and so much to say, that Ryan volunteered, much to Amy and Jimmy's delight, to drive the Smith family back to Boston in the tour bus. Amy quickly accepted the invitation, claiming that it was a much better way to go than the old, cramped, crowded church van.

Ryan handed Annie a cell phone and told her to call the auditorium and have someone locate her friends from church. "We've kept your van crew waiting long enough," Ryan smiled charmingly at Annie. "Just tell them that you're getting a lift home from your brother in law."

After Annie made the call, she settled down on the couch next to Ryan. She appeared unusually serious and quiet, and Ryan asked her what was wrong.

"I just feel like it's asking an awful lot of you to bring us all the way back to Boston. It's a good two hours from here."

"Relax," Ryan dropped an arm around Annie's shoulders and gave her a quick squeeze, "my next concert is in Maine. We'll be driving right through Boston anyway."

"Thank you."

"You're entirely welcome," Ryan replied lightly with a mischievous glimmer in his eyes. "I'll enjoy the ride getting to know about my brother, and," he turned to look directly into Annie's brown eyes, "you."

Annie stared at Ryan intently for a moment. His baby blue eyes met her gaze boldly and held it for several seconds. Annie slowly turned away from him and the staring contest that was going on. She took a moment to gather up her courage and then said carefully but pointedly, "Ryan, I don't mind telling you whatever you want to know about your brother. As for me," Annie cleared her throat loudly, "don't expect to learn much on the personal side. I'm a very private person, and I'd like to keep it that way."

Another staring contest was being held, and this time Annie didn't back down. She felt adamant about her private life staying private. She knew that the sooner Ryan understood this, the better it would be for both of them.

As the stare between them was turning into a glare, Amy let out a loud laugh that broke the scrutinizing confrontation. Ryan looked over at her curiously, with both eyebrows raised invitingly. It was more than obvious that he was encouraging her input on the subject. Annie felt herself cringe inside.

"Yeah," Amy nodded her head, "Mom's very private. She's so tightlipped she could work for the C.I.A.!"

"Amy!" Annie shouted in a disapproving tone. Everyone laughed but Annie. She just sat there with her stomach knotting up inside.

"Well, that can change in time." Ryan didn't even try to hide his amusement.

Annie glared back at him, leaving little doubt as to what she thought about his last comment. "I think we should stick to talking about your brother," she said firmly.

"So," Ryan said entirely too nonchalantly, "let's talk about him. The first thing I want to know is, was he a Christian?"

Annie was relieved that Ryan was focusing in on his brother again and she felt herself begin to relax. "Oh, yes, "Annie smiled, "Ryan was a wonderful Christian man. He accepted Jesus into his life as a child."

"So did I," Ryan nodded. "I was eight."

"He was ten," Annie added warmly. "Ryan was fortunate to grow up in a strong Christian family.

He went to Christian camp as a kid, and than Christian college when he was older."

"Oh yeah," Ryan asked curiously, "which college?"

"He went to Gordon College, just outside of Boston."

"I went to Messiah College in Pennsylvania. That's where I met Kay."

The conversation flowed easily for the next several hours. Even long after the bus had pulled into Annie's Stony Brook Farm, they stayed deep in conversation, trading stories freely.

"So," Ryan asked while folding his hands together, "did your Ryan play any sports?"

Annie nodded. "As a kid he played everything. When he got to college, he was discouraged from playing sports. You see, he was studying to become a music teacher. He had to learn to play many different instruments. If he injured his fingers or hands, he could put his music aspirations in jeopardy."

Ryan shook his head slightly. "Now that's a song I've heard a million times. I loved baseball, but didn't play in college for the same reason."

Ryan paused for a moment and sighed deeply. "I can't believe that he was a music major, and that I was a music major."

Annie smiled tenderly. "The likenesses just keep on coming up."

"OK," Ryan asked with a playful grin on his lightly stubble bearded face, "how was my brother with girls? Was he the flirting kind that had a flock of chicks following him like his own personal harem, or was he a one girl man?"

Annie laughed loudly. "Well that's an easy one. He was definitely a one-girl man. He only dated one girl in high school, and then in college he only dated me. We started dating when I was a freshman and he was a junior. And," Annie sighed dramatically, "we fell deeply in love with each other."

"Now that sounds just like me too."

It started out as a simple grin, but Annie couldn't contain the laughter that was dying to escape from her. It rang out loud and clear, leaving no room for doubt on exactly what she thought of his dating style.

Ryan appeared shocked and outwardly offended. "What? You don't think that I'm the type of guy to stay with just one girl?"

"When you were married, yes," Annie could barely contain her giggles, "but when you were dating, definitely no."

Ryan hung his head and looked at her as though he were a whipped puppy. "I'm not sure how you figure me out to be the Casanova you do, Annie," Ryan said in a very serious tone. "My entire life I only dated three girls, one of whom I married."

The shock written all over Annie's face could not have stood out more if it had been written on with permanent black marker. "Really?" was all she could squeak out in response.

Ryan nodded and then burst out laughing. "Surprised, aren't you?" He was grinning victoriously at her.

Annie stared at him not knowing what to say.

"Annie, I'm a loyal, faithful guy. I've always been serious about dating, and never did it half heartedly."

"Dad hasn't gone on a single date since Mom died." David had come to his father's defense. "That was two years ago. He's got babes practically throwing themselves at him because of his music career, and he always firmly turns them away."

"Yeah," Amy added reflectively, "my mom hasn't dated since my dad died either. She gets asked out a lot, but she says that since she isn't getting married again, she doesn't plan on dating."

"Amy! That's enough!" Annie was appalled. This was one area of her life that she definitely didn't want to discuss with Ryan Jones.

"Never getting married again?" Ryan looked at Annie completely astonished. "Never is a long, lonely time Annie," he eyed her compassionately.

"We're not talking about me. Remember?"

Ryan nodded, but didn't take his intense gaze off her. It was totally unnerving! The man could probably out stare a stone statue.

Annie sighed loudly. "Would you please stop doing that?"

"Doing what?" Ryan asked innocently, as if he honestly didn't have a clue in the world as to what he was doing.

"Stop looking at me so intently! You make me feel like a bug under a microscope...and I just don't like it!"

"I'm sorry, Annie," Ryan sounded absolutely sincere. "I guess I can get a little intense when I'm thinking."

Annie laughed loudly. "That is the understatement of the year Mr. Ryan Jones!" As she looked over at him, she held his gaze for a minute before speaking in a quiet voice. "Please, Ryan," Annie urged, feeling helpless to convey herself as deeply as she wanted to, "please don't try to figure me out. I was so in love with my Ryan, that I could never think of marrying again."

Ryan continued to stare at her thoughtfully. In a frustrated tone, she stated firmly, "Ryan, I can't explain it any better than that, so, you'll just have to accept my explanation. Case closed."

Ryan nodded at her understandingly. "Don't you think that God could bring another godly man into your life? Don't you think that God could bring someone along that you could fall head over heels for and be madly in love with?"

Annie studied Ryan closely for a minute and to her surprise and irritation, she found that he was completely serious. She took a deep breath before answering him. "No," she answered flatly, "end of discussion."

"God can do anything," Ryan persisted gently.

"It would take a miracle," Annie mumbled sarcastically, carefully avoiding Ryan's compassionate eyes.

"Miracles happen every day."

"Not these kinds of miracles," Annie whispered softly, in a defeated tone.

Ryan was wise enough to let the subject drop. He knew it was time to end his inquiry. Pressing Annie any further on this point, at this time, would prove negative. It would simply wind up pushing her away. He knew that Annie's heart needed a miracle, and in some unexplainable way, he also knew that he was going to be part of that miracle.

Four

As Annie invited Ryan, David and Gil into her old, yellow, country farmhouse for coffee, she was surprised to see it was already past midnight. Jimmy quickly said good-bye to the group and headed home, while the rest of the crew settled down around Annie's long rambling oak kitchen table. Annie set steaming cups of coffee and a large plate of homemade chocolate chip cookies in front of them. Everyone seemed too wound up to call it a night, and the conversation continued to flow unhindered, as if they had known each other all their lives.

"So," Ryan asked Amy in an inquisitive tone, "who's Jimmy?"

Amy saw exactly where Ryan was going with his question and laughed loudly. "He's a friend from church and school."

A wide, audacious smile spread slowly across Ryan's face. He made no attempt to hide his curiosity about Amy's friend. "Just a friend, huh?" he echoed back to her in a questioning tone.

Amy laughed again. "Yes, he a friend. Why is it so interesting anyway?"

Ryan's smile grew even wider, as a loud, jolly laugh escaped from his mouth. "I'll tell you why." His tone was light, yet there was no mistaking the serious undercurrents. "I'm your uncle," he stated proudly, "and that gives me certain privileges to interfere in your personal life." He paused for a moment to see if Amy would toss up an argument. When she didn't, he continued on in a matter of fact tone. "I feel it is my responsibility, as your uncle, to make sure that the boys that are interested in you have good intentions. If they don't," amusement flooded his face again, "David and I will personally have to pound them."

The room exploded with laughter, but no one was laughing harder than Amy. It was clear that she found her uncle's words both touching and humorous. "Honest, Uncle Ryan, Jimmy is just a good friend. We have known each other since kindergarten. There is no romance involved. He's really just a friend." Amy paused for a moment as more laughter erupted from her. "And, as for you and David personally pounding him, there's no need. Jimmy's like a brother to me."

Ryan smiled warmly at her. "OK," he nodded his head slightly, obviously satisfied with her explanation. "But," he raised a hand in the air, "if you ever need someone to talk to about boys, or," he wiggled his eyebrows impishly at her, "if you ever need one of them pounded, David and I would be more than happy to help."

David stood up and flexed his muscles and everyone laughed at his antics. Amidst the teasing, Amy received Ryan's message loud and clear. He wanted to start doing the uncle job and he wanted to be there for her.

"Thanks, Uncle Ryan. What you just said means a lot to me, especially since I no longer have a dad, and my brother is away much of the time."

Ryan smiled at her lovingly and winked. "Just keep those teenage boys in the friends category, and we'll get along just fine."

Ryan turned his attention to Annie. He was sitting directly across from her at the table, and it made it very easy for him to spy on her. He began to grow thoughtful and quiet. Annie could feel his concentrated eyes studying her. She hated when he zoomed in on her like that. It made her feel so uncomfortable. She decided the best thing to do was tackle him head on. Nervously tucking some short brown hair behind her ear, she looked at him directly. "What?" she asked, eyeing him carefully.

The corners of his mouth lifted upward in a smile, yet his deep blue eyes continued to look at her thoughtfully. "I'd like to ask you a question, but I don't want to get you upset."

Annie's eyes narrowed as a million different subjects paraded through her mind and none of which she wanted to discuss with the probing Ryan Jones.

"It's better to boldly confront her with your questions, Uncle Ryan," Amy announced smugly, sounding like she was speaking from experience. "It's the only way you'll get anything out of her."

"Amy!" Annie shouted, feeling embarrassment wash over her at her daughter's revelation. Truth was not the issue at the moment, secrecy was. "I think we can live without your expert advice, dear." Annie paused a moment, glancing at the kitchen clock. "By the way, Am, isn't it past your bedtime?" The room ignited in laughter again.

"Oh, Mom," Amy's tone held just the right amount of conviction, pleading her case in a way that would have made any high-powered attorney proud, "you can't make me go to bed now. This is the biggest night of my life! I finally get to meet my uncle, who we've been searching for forever and," Amy smiled impishly at Ryan, "who turns out to be the cute Ryan Jones...my favorite Christian singer!"

Ryan smiled at her and quickly winked. It was clear he found Amy's words amusing. "Thank you."

Then Ryan looked over at Annie with the most incredibly charming smile. "Annie, you can't put her to bed now. She's a fan! Besides," he paused to snag another cookie off the plate, "we've just started to catch up on things. We have a lot of time to make up."

Annie knew when she was outnumbered and right now she definitely was. Even Gil, the big bear of a man, was smiling at her warmly. "Just watch what you say," she pinned her daughter with a stern look.

"C.I.A," Amy mumbled under her breath. The room broke into laughter again. Trying to change the subject, Annie tapped Ryan on the hand. "What did you want to ask me before?"

He nodded, and then said slowly, "You don't have to answer it if it's too personal." He was looking at her seriously, but just a hint of laughter hung in his eyes.

"I didn't say I'd answer it at all," Annie replied quickly, as a big smile spread across her face. "I was simply curious about your question."

Ryan laughed loudly and shook his head. "Annie, you are one tough case." She held his gaze steadily as he gently took her hand. "You shouldn't be so suspicious. It's not a healthy way to approach life."

In a calculated move, Annie slowly pulled her hand away from him and crossed her arms firmly across her chest. "I am not a suspicious person," she proclaimed adamantly.

The entire crew instantly hit the room in laughter as though they had been detonated. "Traitors..." she tried her best to remain serious, but couldn't. "I'm surrounded by a bunch of smart alecs!"

Annie grew serious as she looked back at Ryan. "Listen, seeing you tonight has been difficult in a way." She paused as a troubled sigh escaped from her lips, and she curled her fingers tightly around her coffee cup, as if trying to gather her strength. "It's like you were my Ryan's ghost, or double, or something. It's just so strange. Never in all the years that Ryan and I were together, did I ever see anyone who resembled him as closely as you do." Annie looked up from her coffee cup to find Ryan's compassionate eyes on her. "It just takes a little getting used to," she said feeling lost in his loving eyes for a minute.

Ryan nodded understandingly. "It's been a big night for all of us."

The room quieted for a moment as everyone reflected on the events of the night. Then suddenly Annie asked Ryan, "Oh, you had a question. What was it?"

Ryan's face grew serious, and his eyes contemplative. "I wanted to know how my brother died."

Annie felt a bit startled at first, but then nodded her head. She understood his need to know. He was, after all, his brother. She took a long drink of coffee and then fiddled with her mug before answering. "Ryan died suddenly of a heart attack."

Ryan Jones stared at her in shock. "At forty?" Annie nodded. "People at forty don't die of heart attacks."

"Well, he did." Annie's voice was filled with pain as she thought about her husband's death. "And there was no warning either. One evening he was at the stove, making his famous, secret spaghetti sauce, when he suddenly dropped to the floor." Annie tightened her fingers around her mug, as she felt the emotion of the event rip through her again. "At first, I thought he was joking," Annie's tone sounded like a frightened five-year-old child. She glanced up at Ryan quickly, but turned away from his loving eyes as her own began to fill up with tears.

"Ryan was such a joker. He was always goofing around." Annie paused to study her coffee again, as she fought to control her tears. They refused to subside and began to spill out of the corners of her eyes, and race down her cheeks. She closed her eyes and shook her head slowly as she thought about the evening. It had just been too much. Once again she felt overwhelmed by the terrible memories.

Annie jumped a mile as she felt an arm come around her shoulders. Her eyes flew open and her head snapped to the left, only to find Ryan sitting next to her with his arm tenderly around her. His eyes were filled with tears and the expression on his face was an angelic combination of love, sorrow, and compassion.

He pulled Annie into his big arms. She let her face rest on his chest, while her deep sobs shook her entire body. The pain and the hurt that she seemed unable to express verbally, just rolled out freely through her tears. Ryan held her tenderly, running a soothing hand through her light brown hair.

When Annie's tears subsided, she began to pull away awkwardly from Ryan's arms. "I'm so sorry." She suddenly felt embarrassed and self-conscious. "I don't usually do that."

Ryan took a few napkins from the table and handed them to Annie. As she wiped her face, he spoke to her from his heart. "Annie, I know what it's like to lose someone that you love more than life itself. Kay was my wife and best friend. She was such a huge part of me." He stopped for a second, sighing loudly as he ran a hand through his brown hair. "I have never known such great heart wrenching pain in my entire life." He paused again and looked down at Annie lovingly. "I've cried in the daytime, in the nighttime, and even in my dreams."

He cleared his throat, and then continued. "I think you've done a lot of crying on the inside Annie. It's past due that you let it all out. Don't be afraid to cry. God heals us through our tears."

Annie nodded thoughtfully. "I know," she admitted in a soft voice. "Without God's help, I never would have made it this far."

Everyone was quiet for a minute, until Amy said thoughtfully, "One of the hardest things about losing my dad was the way he seemed healthy as a horse. He had even had his yearly physical the week before. The doctor told him he was in great shape."

"Really?" Ryan turned to Annie in alarm.

Annie nodded slowly. "That's why I insisted that they do an autopsy on him. None of it made any sense to me. I simply had to know what had happened." She paused for a minute and exhaled loudly. "I knew that I'd never have a moment's peace until I knew the reason for Ryan's death."

Ryan looked at her intently. "Did the autopsy reveal anything unusual?"

Annie nodded reflectively. "Yes," she answered in a distant voice, "the doctors discovered that Ryan had a condition known as HOCM. It stands for Hypertrophic Obstructive Cardiomyopathy. It's a rare genetic disorder that can cause apparently healthy people to suddenly die. It was unable to be detected in his regular check-up's. He had absolutely no warning."

Ryan Jones leaned over and put a loving arm around Annie. "That's enough for now." His tone was both loving and protective. "I think we should change the subject."

Annie nodded in agreement as she casually glanced around the table. Everyone's eyes were clouded with tears. Annie closed her eyes for a minute, trying to push all the painful memories away.

Just then, a thought struck her hard and she stiffened. Ryan slipped his arm away from her and looked at her with a concerned expression. "What's wrong?"

Annie pushed her chair away from the table and slowly got up. "Wait a minute…" She appeared lost in deep thought. She knew she was on the verge of putting something together, but she didn't have a clue as to what yet. Her tired mind was running in slow mode. She began to pace the kitchen; oblivious to the curious stares she was receiving. "Ryan's mother…" Annie stated slowly, "your mother…" she waved a hand toward Ryan, "died of a heart attack." She paused and let the thought hang in the air for a second. "My Ryan died unexpectedly of a heart attack." Once again, her words hung heavy in the air. "You know," Annie snapped her fingers together, "I just bet it's hereditary!" Again she paused and then ran her fingers through her short brown hair. "And, if it's hereditary," she targeted Ryan with her eyes, "you may be at risk too!"

With a faint move of his shoulders he seemed to all but dismiss the charges. He was not even concerned enough about what she had just said to verbally reply to it. It infuriated Annie, and she felt her temper starting to rise.

"Ryan," she addressed him firmly, sounding very much like an irritated schoolteacher, "I'm serious about this."

"Annie," Ryan held up his hands toward her, "I know where you're going with this, and, I'm fine." Ryan smiled slightly, his eyes lighting with humor. "I'm as healthy as they come."

"So was your brother," Annie shot back instantly.

"Annie, I've just had my yearly poke and prod. My doctors say that I'm fine."

"So did my husband's!" Annie pointed out angrily as she marched across the room toward Ryan.

Ryan got up to meet his attacker and crossed his arms firmly over his broad chest. They were having their first real argument, and both of them looked as stubborn as two bulls.

"Annie," Ryan's tone was completely unyielding, "I'm not going to see any more doctors for a while. Every time I check in for my yearly physical, the media informs the entire planet."

Annie faced him fearlessly. With her hands planted on her hips, she spoke in a tight voice, "So, just because you're afraid of what the papers will say about you, you're not going to get checked out! That's irresponsible and just plain stupid!"

"Annie," Ryan groaned, with definite annoyance rising in his voice, "I understand your fears. What you're feeling is quite normal. But," he waved a finger at her, with an obnoxious smirk plastered across his stubborn face, "I'm fine. Leave it alone."

Fat chance, she thought as she took another step toward him. She wasn't about to back down now. She had a point to prove, and she aimed to do so. As her 5'4" frame dwarfed next to Ryan's 6'2" height, she stood her ground firmly. "You!" she stuck a finger into his chest angrily, "are the most pig-headed, stubborn man I've ever met! I don't know how on earth you can ever speak when your mouth is so full of arrogance, pride, and conceit!"

Ryan's face broke into a wide grin and his eyes lighted proudly, as though Annie had just given him the greatest compliment in the world.

"Don't you see," the frustration was mounting in Annie's voice and the tears started rolling down her cheeks, "people who have HOCM normally feel fine. They usually don't have a bunch of symptoms to warn them that something is wrong. It's a silent killer, and you never know when it's going to strike. They die suddenly of a heart attack. But you," Annie said in a choked up voice, "you're one of the lucky ones. You're being given a warning. You're getting a second chance that your brother never had. Please see Ryan's doctor tomorrow," Annie begged. "He's the best in Boston. The tests will only take a few hours of your time."

Ryan grew thoughtful and serious as he brushed away Annie's tears. As he was studying her closely, something softened in his eyes. Annie noticed it and went in for the kill. "Ryan, it just may save your life."

It was the first time that she had used his name with so much love in her voice and for some reason it affected him deeply. The sight of his sister-in-law, pleading before him in tears, stirred him in a way that he had not been moved for a long time. He took Annie's hand and pulled her into a loving embrace. She had already become so precious to him. "Listen, Annie," Ryan said softly, "I promise you I'll think about it."

Annie didn't like his answer one bit and pushed him immediately away. He stared at her and chuckled quietly. Annie just glared back. She was steaming.

"Don't be so angry."

"I'd like to flatten you!"

"Could prove interesting," Ryan challenged, with a wicked grin plastered across his face.

"Dad," a quiet voice broke through their argument. Ryan looked across the room toward his son. "Dad," David repeated again louder this time, "I think you should go for the tests. It makes a lot of sense to me, and," David paused for a minute to fight the growing emotion building up inside of him, "Dad, we already lost Mom too soon. I can't bare to lose you too."

Ryan went quickly across the room and embraced his son in a big loving hug. After a minute he released his son but kept a firm arm around his shoulders. "What?" Ryan asked as he scanned the room. "All of you agree with her? This is ridiculous!" He paused a moment looking for someone to come to his rescue, but none came. "You're all ganging up on me," Ryan tried to be humorous. No one laughed. "Listen," he waved a hand passively at the group, "it's late, and everyone's tired. Why don't we discuss this in the morning?"

Then Ryan turned back to Annie. "Do you have some place where we could crash for the night? The bus is too small to hold us all, and it's late."

Annie glanced at the large kitchen clock on the wall and gasped. It was already two in the morning. Time had flown. Annie looked back at Ryan's tired face and began to grow panicky.

Ryan saw the look and looked like he was barely able to contain his laughter. "Annie," he said in a friendly but amused tone, "I don't bite!" Everyone in the room laughed at his joke except for Annie.

"You're like a stranger to me,"Annie blurted out nervously. "I don't really know you."

Ryan stepped forward and gently touched her shoulders. Every time he touched her, he seemed to reach down to her very core. Annie quickly tried to pack away the feeling he arose in her. She needed more time than she presently had to sort through her emotional mess. She felt that her emotional state was completely out of whack since she had met Ryan. She didn't want to blame it on him. She felt she was probably going through some sort of a mid-life crisis, that she was consciously, and probably subconsciously denying. She was good at denial. She knew that if she was denying this consciously, then she was definitely denying it subconsciously as well. She stayed together with her denials. She would figure it all out later, or at least enough of it to consciously deny that she was in any sort of crisis at all.

"Annie," Ryan looked at her kindly, "after all the heart to heart talking we've done here tonight, I feel like you know me better than most."

Annie exhaled loudly and began to relax a little. It was true. They had talked about a lot of heart-felt issues tonight. They had opened up to each other and shared with each other freely. She did know that Ryan Jones was a man of God. There was no denying this fact. Annie smiled. Actually, that wasn't the fact she was working so hard to deny. What she was having the most trouble admitting, and no trouble denying at all were the feelings that she was beginning to have for Ryan. Annie smiled again. If she didn't deal with these feelings that she was having, both consciously and subconsciously, all this denial was going to lead to a great deal of therapy.

"Listen," Annie smiled mischievously, "you're welcome to our guest room on one condition."

Ryan met her mischievous grin with one of his own. "Yeah, and just what is your condition, Little Lady?"

"You'll have to see the doctor in the morning," Annie's tone was completely serious now. "You don't have to go for the tests unless he recommends them."

"You know," Ryan eyed the group wearily, "there's going to be no living with any of you until I go see the doctor. I might as well just save myself from future badgering and just go."

A cheer went up from the crowd and Annie gave Ryan a quick hug. "Would you please point me toward a pillow. I'm beyond exhausted. I'm standing on the edge of the twilight zone." He smiled, gave her a quick squeeze, and released her.

"Amy," she called out playfully, "would you please get the bedding for the barn? I'm going to head out there now and start to get things set up."

"THE BARN!" Ryan's complete look of shock was comical to say the very least. "I'm agreeing to see a doctor that I don't want to see, in exchange for a night's sleep in a barn! You have got to be kidding, Annie."

"Not at all," Annie smiled back at him.

"Can't we negotiate here, Annie?" Ryan begged in a hopefully. "The couch would be fine, even the living room floor."

"You'll like the barn better."

"Listen, I have a barn back in Chatfield Hollow, Tennessee. I know what barns are like. I can tell you right now, without a shadow of a doubt, I am definitely not going to like the barn better."

"You'll like this barn. Trust me."

Ryan turned toward Amy, and said teasing, "She's not very hospitable, is she?"

Everyone laughed and then Annie nudged Ryan toward the back door. "Just follow me," she grinned like a Cheshire cat. Annie waved a hand at David and Gil and told them to follow. As she turned the back porch light on and they marched off toward the barn, the men were grumbling like a bunch of tired, unhappy children.

The red and white classic New England styled barn would be seen glowing in the yard lights. Annie and her late husband had converted half of the large barn into a guest cottage. Three small bedrooms, complete with pine bunk beds, built right into the walls, held twelve people comfortably. A small bathroom, with a shower and a living room/dining room occupied the rest of the cottage. She knew that if she had shared this small little detail with Ryan earlier, it would have eliminated his doubts about sleeping in the barn. She was quickly coming to realize how much she really did enjoy teasing him.

As they entered the barn, Annie couldn't help but laugh at the surprised and relieved expressions that spread across the men's faces. "Now, you didn't honestly think that your new sister-in-law was going to put you out to sleep in the hay with the cows, did you?"

The grunts and groans of laughter could be heard from the men. Ryan walked over to Annie and put a loving arm around her shoulders. "You know," he looked at her clearly amused, "you could have told me the barn was a finished guest room."

"Yeah," Annie laughed, "I could have. I thought you'd enjoy the surprise."

Ryan groaned. "You're an imp. Letting me think that I was going to sleep with the cows was not kind of you. If you keep this up, I'm going to have to start to think of ways to repay you for your kindness."

"Aw, you don't need to repay me."

"Yes, Annie," Ryan laughed, "I really think I do. You're a troublemaker."

"Who? Me?" Annie asked wide-eyed and innocently.

Ryan smiled. "You can't pull that Miss Innocent routine with me. It's too late Annie. I've already got your number."

Annie laughed. "What you've got is a wrong number."

"We'll see." Ryan winked at her and then looked around the cottage. "You guys did an incredible job in here. This place is great."

"Yes, and no cows!" Annie giggled.

"Very funny," Ryan eyed her mischievously.

Amy arrived a moment later with an armload of sheets and old quilts. Together, the mother/ daughter team went to work making up three bunks. Just as they finished, they heard a growl, and then a scream from the den area. Annie and Amy ran to find Ranger and Scout, standing in the doorway, growling at the three men. The male shepherds, at one hundred pounds apiece, made a very unwelcoming sight as they snarled their teeth at the visitors.

"Ranger! Scout!" Annie commanded in an authoritative voice, "No!" The large dogs looked at Annie as if she were totally unaware of the fact that three strangers were standing in the room.

Annie laughed at the dog's confused expressions and her voice softened. "Come here, boys. It's alright." Reluctantly the dogs obeyed and trudged over to Annie. She lovingly stroked their tan and black heads as she talked to them. "Ranger, Scout, I'd like you to meet Ryan, David, and Gil." Then in an impish voice she added, "And please don't bite them tonight. I'm not planning on going to the doctor's until tomorrow."

"That's very funny, Annie," Ryan said sarcastically as he eyed the dogs wearily. "You're a ball of laughs."

"You don't need to be afraid of them now. They understand that you're our guests here. They'll be fine with you."

"That's easy for you to say," Ryan complained uneasily, noticing that the shepherds had both not taken their eyes off him. They were still on guard duty, and he felt that he was likely to be their first midnight snack. "You're not being stared at by two hundred pounds of teeth."

"Mom," Amy asked suddenly, "do you think that Ranger and Scout notice the resemblance between Daddy and Ryan?"

Annie nodded thoughtfully. "Probably, Am. Shepherds are very intelligent dogs. They're probably trying to figure out what's going on."

"Uh, I don't mean this in the culinary sense," Ryan stated in a concerned voice, "but did the dogs like your husband?"

Annie laughed. "I see where you're coming from. Yes, they adored Ryan, and not in the culinary sense." Annie laughed again. "They would follow Ryan around all day, and they slept by the foot of our bed at night. You really shouldn't have anything to worry about."

"Shouldn't…" Ryan's voice filled with concern as he stared at the huge dogs. "That word is not at all comforting."

"You'll be fine." Annie patted Ryan on the back. "You look like you're in good shape. How fast can you run?" Annie couldn't contain her laughter.

"You're going to give me nightmares, Annie. This is not a good bedtime story."

"I'm just teasing you. I'll bring the dogs in the house with me. You have nothing to worry about."

"I'm still not encouraged. I think I'll sleep on a top bunk just in case they decide to visit me in the night."

This idea seemed to ease Ryan's mind until David hastily asked, "They can't climb the ladder to the top bunk, can they, Aunt Annie?"

Annie hesitated just momentarily, but it was long enough for them to get their answer without her saying anything.

"Dad, you can have any top bunk you want, I'm sleeping on the bus." David grabbed a pillow and headed for the door.

Amy blocked the doorway. "Don't be such a chicken. The dogs will be in the house with us. They sleep in my mom's room every night. They don't want to be in the barn. You don't need to worry. Besides, it's not like they bite. "Well," Amy began to backpeddle, "at least not often. Only when they have to...I mean, well, they are German Shepherds."

"Oh, this is just great." David looked over to his father for help.

"Listen," Annie's voice was honest and sincere, "the dogs have never ever bitten a guest. I'm taking them to the house with me now. You won't see them until breakfast." Annie sighed loudly. "I promise you'll be fine." A smile crept slowly across Annie's face, and Ryan immediately picked up on it.

"What's with the smile?" Ryan asked suspiciously. "You say words of comfort and then you smile like that and it totally erases any comfort that I had."

Annie laughed. "The dogs won't bother you, but we have had a pesky old skunk coming around here at night. He's trigger-happy and shoots quickly. I would strongly recommend not going outside at night, or early dawn, unless you have to. If you do go out, be careful."

All the men looked at her in disbelief. "Listen," Annie said wearily, "it is autumn in New England, and that brings out the skunks. I would rather run into just about any animal in the woods than a skunk. They frightened easily, and shoot quickly."

The men just continued to stared at her. "It's late. Hop into a bunk and get some sleep. We'll wake you in the morning."

After Annie and Amy said good night to their anxious guests, they headed back to the house, with the dogs in tow. Annie couldn't help but think about the events of the day. The day had been more than full, and suddenly she felt very overwhelmed with fatigue. As she climbed into bed, she absent-mindedly reached down to pat Ranger and Scout. She wanted to make sure they were in the room. If they had gone back to the barn, she knew the dogs would not appreciate their houseguests. Annie laughed quietly as she thought that the houseguests would definitely not appreciate the dogs either. They would get to know each other tomorrow, Annie thought exhaustedly. Tomorrow would have a whole new set of adventures for her, and she felt too exhausted to tackle any of them right now.

Five

The next morning, Annie quietly woke Ryan up at 8:00 A.M. "It's too early!" he complained in a groggy voice, sounding very much like a grumbling black bear. "We were up half the night; I'd planned on sleeping in half the morning."

"Well," Annie said cheerfully, trying not to notice how handsome he was first thing in the morning, "you have an appointment with Dr. Thatcher in an hour."

Ryan's eyes widened and Annie laughed. For some reason she took great pleasure in throwing the calm, cool, collected Ryan Jones off balance just a little.

"We need to leave here in half an hour." Annie paused looking at her watch. "So, if you want to take a shower, you'd better move it."

Ryan playfully sniffed under his arms. "I don't smell too bad. Come back and wake me up in an hour."

Annie couldn't help but laugh at him. "We're leaving in half an hour," she stated as sternly as she could, "and I strongly suggest that you take a shower. It's that way." Annie pointed her finger toward the small bathroom.

"Does that mean that you think I stink?" Ryan asked humorously. Annie dramatically took two fingers and pinched her nose closed. Ryan's mouth dropped open, pretending to be shocked. Annie laughed softly and shook her head.

"Oh, I've put a bunch of razors in the bathroom cabinet for you." Ryan looked at her puzzled but amused.

"I just assumed that your razor must have broken. Every picture that I've ever seen of you," she paused searching for the right words, "well, you have a serious case of six o'clock shadow on your face."

Ryan laughed. "Are you referring to my closely cut beard?"

Annie laughed loudly. "That's not a beard, that's stubble!"

"It's called fashion."

Annie smiled. He looked like he was trying hard to act insulted, but the laughter playing around the corners of his mouth gave him away.

"It's called fuzz," she laughed openly at him. "If you take ten minutes to clear that forest off your face, you'll feel so much better!" Annie could still hear his laughter as she walked back to the house.

Twenty minutes later, a showered and shaved Ryan Jones appeared before her in the kitchen. He was wearing a white plain tee shirt, new stone washed jeans, and a navy wool blazer. Annie stopped dead in her tracks and stared at him for a solid second. Then, shaking her head at him, she simply smiled. Ryan Jones was an incredibly handsome man, just as her Ryan had been. His hair seemed to know exactly where it needed to go to look great, and his eyes looked even bluer this morning, though a sleepy haze hung over them. The two brothers were given an overdose in the appearance department. They not only had all the right stuff, they knew how to carry it off in an entirely charming way.

"So," Annie felt full of energy and mischief this morning, "this must be the look that makes your female fans swoon and drop at your feet!"

Ryan's eyes lit with amusement and a totally charming smile spread quickly across his handsome, cleanly shaven face. He unbuttoned his sports jacket and did a quick twirl for her. "Are you swooning yet?" he asked her entertainingly.

"No, but I'm your sister-in-law. I think that must give me a certain immunity to your powers!" Annie laughed outwardly, but on the inside she was dying. Ryan Jones was such a special man that he was enough to make her start thinking seriously.

He was enough to make her start worrying. He was more than enough to put a gnawing pain of fear in the pit of her stomach. He was throwing her well-ordered world off balance and breaking through her armored walls of protection like they were made of Jello. She had been so careful to protect her heart, and he had so easily started to penetrate his way through.

She needed a distraction and she needed one quickly. She grabbed three blueberry muffins from a basket on the counter. She proceeded to throw them across the kitchen at Ryan in rapid-fire succession.

"Hey! Hey! Hang on! I'm not awake!" Ryan was definitely dissatisfied with the style that his breakfast was being served. Annie couldn't help but smile.

"Your breakfast, Sir." Annie used her best British accent, while bowing toward him slightly. "Oh," she quickly turned back toward the counter, "and here's your coffee."

"You're not going to throw that at me too, are you?" Ryan asked with sudden panic growing in his voice.

Annie just about fell over laughing as she grabbed Ryan's arm and tugged him toward the door. "Come on, good looking." She handed him a mug of black coffee. "We don't want to keep the doctor waiting."

As Annie swerved her Chevy Blazer in and out of the heavy Boston morning rush hour traffic, Ryan braced himself in his seat with both hands. A knot was steadily growing in his stomach, and he began to feel that his breakfast was about to volcano up all over Annie's car.

"Annie," Ryan's voice was dripping with tension and anxiety, "it's a good thing that we're on our way to the doctor's, because your driving is going to get us severely injured or quite possibly killed."

Annie smiled and glanced at Ryan for a second. "Hey there, Country Boy, you're not used to the rush hour traffic in a big city, are you? It can get pretty crowded." She reached over and patted his leg like he was four years old. "Don't worry; you're in good hands. I'm a pro at this."

"The crowd is not what's bothering me," Ryan's tone was irritated. "You're driving is crazy. You just changed lanes back there and there was no room. The other car was right on top of us."

"There was plenty of room." Annie blew off his concern. "I had at least a quarter of an inch," Annie said playfully. "That's more than enough."

Ryan couldn't keep quiet. The fear mounting in him was motivating him to try to reason with this Nascar-want-to-be crazed woman. He had never driven with anyone like her in his life, and if he survived this ordeal, he hoped he never would again. "Why do you think that the driver you cut in front of was waving his fist at you and blowing his horn?"

"He wasn't waving his fist, Ryan, he was waving his hand. I've lived in Boston all my life. It was probably someone I knew just saying hi."

"Annie," Ryan was heated now, "people don't blow their horns on the highway to say hi."

"I blow my horn all the time on the highway," Annie replied defensively. "Sometimes I'm saying hi, and other times I'm saying get out of my way."

Feeling hopeless, Ryan closed his eyes for a moment. He was trapped in a speeding car with a crazy driver. He knew he was going to die. "Do you think you could slow down for a while? Maybe drive in the right lane for a mile or two?" he asked. The hope in his voice went completely unnoticed by Annie. "I'm getting car sick."

"Ryan, if I slow down, we'll be late for your appointment," Annie stated in a matter-of-fact tone.

"I can live with that. Just slow down. There's a break in traffic now. If you want to change over to the right lane, it's a good time."

Annie glared at Ryan quickly and then focused back on her race. "Ryan, you're asking too much.

You not only want me to slow down, you want me to drive in the right lane, too. I only drive in the right lane when I'm getting ready to exit." Annie glanced at Ryan quickly, "I'm not ready to exit. Stop telling me how to drive or I'll lock you in the trunk."

"You don't have a trunk." Ryan watched another car in his side mirror that Annie had just cut off. She was a complete menace. "Have you ever heard of road rage?" Annie glared at him. "You've created a whole new definition of it. There are at least ten cars behind you that you have cut off, and I'm quite sure those people are majorly ticked off at you."

"Listen, this is Boston. You need to drive aggressively or you'll get run over."

"There is a huge difference between driving aggressively and driving like a total lunatic." Ryan ran a shaky hand through his hair. "You're driving places you in the second category-no question about it."

"I don't want to talk anymore."

"That's OK. Neither do I. If you hear mumbling from my side of the car, it's just me making out a verbal living will. I have a feeling I'm going to need it soon," Ryan sighed loudly. He needed to remember to grab the keys next time before she did. If he survived this incident, he was not going to consciously put himself through it ever again. He could just feel the gray hair popping up all over his head.

When they reached the parking lot, Ryan flew out of the Blazer like a man that had been freed from jail. It was a great relief to get out of the car, and an even greater relief to realize that he had survived the rush hour ride from the land of pure misery and torture. No amusement park ride could have matched what he had just been through.

As Ryan starting taking a good look around him, his stress returned in full force. "I thought you said we were going to the doctor's office? This is a big city hospital."

Annie smiled sympathetically. "Dr. George Thatcher has his office in the hospital. Don't worry," Annie smiled at him sweetly, "just like you, Dr. Thatcher doesn't bite." Annie smirked at Ryan as she quoted his own line back to him. There is nothing like being able to throw someone's own quote right back at him, Annie thought as she grabbed her pocketbook from the Blazer.

"Very funny, Annie." Ryan looked at the blueberry muffin he was holding in his hand. He had forgotten it was there. During the stressful ride into the city, the baseball-sized muffin had been pressurized down to the size of a very compact ping-pong ball. As nonchalantly as he could, he let the wad of muffin drop onto the pavement. It would give the seagulls hanging around the parking lot a real challenge to break the thing apart.

They took the elevator up to the twelfth floor and walked silently to Dr. Thatcher's office. After they had taken their seats in the waiting room, Annie started rummaging through her pocketbook.

"Lose something?" Ryan asked in an amused tone.

"Oh," Annie grumbled as she looked intently through her pocketbook, "I must have left my book in the Blazer. I'll be right back."

As Annie got up and headed for the door, Ryan jumped up. "You're not leaving me here, are you?"

Annie took a few steps back toward him. She could see the concern written all over his face. "Ryan," she said as she touched his arm lightly, "I'll be right back."

"Then I'll go with you."

"No, No," Annie waved a hand at him, "Dr. Thatcher may call you in at any time. I'll be right back."

Reluctantly, Ryan dropped back down into his chair, and Annie hurried out the door. She raced down to her Blazer, grabbed her book, which had slid under her seat, and was back in the office in record time.

As she looked over to where Ryan had been sitting, she was surprised to find his chair empty. She immediately approached the receptionist's desk and inquired.

"Yes," the young woman behind the desk said, "Ryan Jones has been taken to room number 4. Go ahead and join him."

Annie walked down the gray-carpeted floor until she reached room 4. She knocked on the door and Ryan, in a serious and extremely quiet voice said to come in. Annie slowly opened the door and saw him sitting on the examining table wearing the standard hospital gown.

"Can you believe this?" Ryan sounded completely exasperated. "Your doctor is making me wear this dress! I knew I shouldn't have come here."

"Ryan," Annie could barely contain her laughter, "it's not a dress. It's a hospital examination gown."

"Dress...gown," Ryan complained as he sat stiffly on the examination table, "it's all the same thing, Annie, and you know it!"

Annie couldn't seem to stop the big smile that spread across her face. She tried to look away from Ryan so he wouldn't see it, but she wasn't quick enough.

"Oh, so you think this is funny?"

"Ryan, the hospital gown is not funny, but you are."

Ryan groaned loudly but continued on. "The nurse instructed me to take everything off! Everything! You understand where I'm coming from here? I've been stripped down to my birthday suit."

"Happy Birthday!" Annie said cheerfully with a big, toothy smile on her face.

"You're not funny, Annie! I don't want to be here. I hate doctors and I hate hospitals. They make me a nervous wreck."

She could see that Ryan was genuinely worried, and she immediately sought to put his mind at ease. "You should rest assured that Dr. Thatcher is an excellent doctor. He has a wonderful reputation. He won't put you through any unnecessary testing."

Ryan stared at her a minute and then sighed loudly. He looked back down at his hospital gown and said disgustedly, "I am not the type of guy that wears dresses. And besides that, I think mine is broken. Do you know that this thing doesn't even close in the back? If I have to get up to go to the men's room, my naked backside is going to be waving at everyone as I pass! Talk about a major design flaw. This," he touched the gown with distain "is embarrassing. I know embarrassing when I see it, Annie, and this is it!"

Annie fought hard to suppress her laughter, but she just wasn't able to do a very good job of it. "Do you need to use the men's room?" she asked him directly.

"No," Ryan answered in a sulking tone, sounding very much like an unhappy two year old.

"Then you don't need to worry about anyone seeing your backside waving at them as you pass by." Annie was giggling like a schoolgirl.

"I'm glad that you're enjoying this," Ryan moped, acting as though he were positively offended. "If I move, this dress is going to fall apart. I don't think I can hold all the openings together."

Annie laughed. "If I were you, I'd concentrate on the areas that could prove the most embarrassing if they did open. What you're wearing there takes a bit of strategy and planning if you're going to be moving in it."

"If I have to move in this dress, Annie," Ryan smirked at her, "I can guarantee you it's not going to be a pretty picture."

"Hey! Now that's an idea. This could be quite a photo opportunity."

Ryan simply glared at her.

"No, really," she waved a hand in his direction, "all the pictures that your fans get to see of you are those glamour shots of you looking all gorgeous like a model. This would be…. different."

"I'm not posing for anyone in this stupid dress," Ryan stated emphatically.

"Just a thought…" Annie smiled at him. "Let me know if you change your mind."

"You must be out of your mind!" Ryan laughed at her. "But, I have to say, you did manage to take my mind off things. Thanks."

"Always glad to help." Annie shrugged and then turned toward the door. Before she could reach the handle, Ryan asked in a voice full of alarm where she was going.

"You know," she turned back toward him with a mischievous grin plastered across her face, "I think I have my camera in the Blazer. This really is a photo opportunity that's just too hard to pass up. I bet I could sell the pictures to one of those cheap tabloid papers and make a bundle!" Annie exited the room quickly laughing at Ryan's shocked expression.

A few minutes later Annie returned with Ryan's pants. She threw them at him from the door. "The doctor says you can wear your jeans if you're more comfortable."

"Gee," Ryan muttered cynically, "what would I rather wear? My own cool stone washed jeans, or this little feminine drafty dress? I'll have to think about that, Annie."

"Let me know if you opt for the dress, because I think I have a pair of pumps at home that would look great with it."

"You are beyond a pain. You know that?" Ryan laughed at her.

"Thanks," Annie smiled coyly at him. "I'll be back when you've changed."

As Annie stood in the hallway, waiting for Ryan to change, she kept breaking into laughter every time she thought about his "backside worries". "So, not only is Ryan very handsome, with a kind and tender heart, he's as funny as my Ryan was too." She shook her head slightly, trying to shake the similarities from her mind. "He's my brother-in-law," she scolded herself, "and that's all."

Yet deep down inside, when Annie was being totally honest with herself, she knew that the categorizing of Ryan Jones wasn't completely easy or a closed case. The problem was that her mind had him in one category and her heart had him in another. He was her brother-in-law, which was definitely true. Yet, there was just some special way that her heart connected with his that she couldn't quite deny either. She tried too. She tried not to think about how attracted she was to him, yet it was becoming harder and harder to convince herself.

Emphatically she made a promise to herself. Whatever this all too familiar feeling was that was rustling around in her heart, she promised herself, under no circumstances would she act on those feelings. It would be selfish to do so. She never, ever wanted to be in a relationship again. And, more importantly, because she was beginning to care for Ryan Jones, she felt even more determined not to hurt him.

"Just friends," she repeated firmly to herself. "We are simply just very good friends. That's all."

Annie went back down the hall and knocked on Ryan's door again. Ryan yelled to come in and as she slowly opened the door, she stopped dead in her tracks. Ryan was sitting on the examining table, wearing his jeans, but not the hospital gown. She scanned the room quickly for it and saw it lying in a ball in the corner.

"I'm not putting that dress back on!" Ryan protested in a strong determined tone that left no room for negotiating.

Annie tried not to stare at him, but her heart was beating erratically at the sight of him. Her reaction to him frightened her. What kind of power did this man have over her that he could turn an intelligent, capable woman into a pool of mush? Annie bit her lip hard, silently repeating her earlier declaration. "Just friends, we are just friends, that's all. Really, that's all." Yet somehow the words seemed completely hollow this time.

"I'll be right back." Annie blurted out the words quickly, making a speedy exit from the room. She returned a minute later with Ryan's white tee shirt, and threw it at him.

He looked at the shirt for a minute and then at Annie. "Why do I need to put this on?" Surprise was clearly written across his clueless face. Annie groaned inwardly.

"Because," Annie said as strongly as she could, "I'm not sitting in a room with you when you're only half dressed."

The light went on for Ryan and a knowing smile crept slowly across his face. Annie wanted to die she felt so embarrassed. "Listen, Annie," Ryan began calmly, never taking his probing eyes off her, "this is more than I wear at the beach."

"We're not at the beach, Ryan," Annie replied uncomfortably, as she made it a point to rummage through her pocketbook, looking for absolutely nothing. A big rock to climb under would have been great, she thought, shaking her head at the situation she was in and wishing for an escape route.

"OK," Ryan relaxed for the first time since he'd entered the doctor's office, "I'll put my shirt on. I don't want my muscular chest to make you feel uncomfortable."

Annie still didn't look at him. She felt too embarrassed to do so, not to mention the fact that he had hit the nail right on the head. She could try to deny it, but Ryan was right. She didn't want to look at his muscular chest, yet her eyes seemed glue to it, unable to focus anywhere else. She was here to help him, not swoon over him like some sort of star-struck fan. "Get a grip, girl!" she scolded herself silently. "You have to get it together."

Just then Dr. Thatcher came into the room. "Annie!" he said excitedly, "how are you doing?"

"Fine, George," she answered warmly, thankful for the distraction from Ryan's inquisitive eyes. The doctor was a close family friend, and it was good to see him again. "How's Margaret doing?"

"Margaret's fine," he nodded his head thoughtfully. "Though," he pointed a finger at her, "she still wants you to go on that double date with us. She's very persistent about it."

Annie glanced over at Ryan, and to her dismay, noticed that he was enjoying the conversation far too much. "No thanks, George. Like I said before, I'm not interesting in dating." Annie took a deep breath and blew it out loudly. "Let me introduce you to my brother-in-law."

Dr. Thatcher stared at Ryan Jones a second before saying anything. "Well," his tone was friendly as he reached out to shake Ryan's hand, "it really is

remarkable how much you resemble Ryan Smith."
He paused for a moment and then said with
astonishment, "Smith and Jones - can you believe
that?" Annie and Ryan just smiled at each other.

Then Dr. Thatcher's tone became completely
serious and Annie knew it was time to get down to
business. The doctor carefully explained to Ryan
the unusual heart condition that his twin brother
had. "HOCM is a rare genetic disorder. It causes
seemingly healthy people to die suddenly of
apparent heart problems with little warning."

"Yeah, but what are the chances that I would
have this?" Ryan asked skeptically. "Just because
my brother had it, doesn't make me a candidate for
it. Does it?"

"Actually, it makes you the perfect candidate,"
Dr. Thatcher stated seriously. "Since your twin
brother died of HOCM, I would immediately
suspect that you might have this condition. If an
identical twin has HOCM, the other twin would
have a 100% chance of having the disease. If the
twins are fraternal, then they would have a 50%
chance of having HOCM."

Dr. Thatcher paused for a minute and looked
over at Annie. "Didn't you tell me that the twins
were adopted at birth and have very little medical
history?"

Annie nodded. "Yes. We don't even know for sure if they are fraternal or identical twins. The adoption was a long time ago and their medical history is sketchy at best. Many areas of their history were never completed at all. All we know for sure is that they are twin brothers."

"Well," Dr Thatcher looked thoughtfully at Ryan, "I'd say that you stand to have at least a 50% chance of having this disease. My recommendation is that we get some testing done immediately."

Ryan's jaw swung opened and he stared at the doctor for a moment. "I'm sorry," he ran a nervous hand through his hair. "I'm in complete shock. I really didn't think I stood a chance at having this."

"It's a good thing that Annie dragged you in here," Dr. Thatcher looked over at Annie for a second. "It's very unusual to perform testing for this disease. Most people die from it and it's not discovered until the autopsy."

Ryan nodded thoughtfully. "What tests are you planning to run on me?"

"First we'll do an EKG to obtain an echocardiogram. This is an ultrasound of the heart and should give us enough information to make a diagnosis."

"That sounds simple enough." Relief flowed from Ryan's voice. "And, if I do have HOCM, what can you do about it?"

"People with HOCM can be treated with medicine, which would be beta blockers or with surgical procedures. If your condition requires surgery, I would be inserting an internal cardiac defibrillator into your chest."

"Is that like a pacemaker?" Ryan asked in a confused voice.

"Yes," Dr. Thatcher's tone was reassuring. "It's very similar to a pace- maker. Instead of controlling the rate of your heart, the ICD provides a small amount of electrical current to the heart if an abnormal or dangerous rhythm is detected."

"OK," Ryan nodded thoughtfully. "Could you tell me exactly what you're going to be looking for during the EKG?"

"I'll perform an EKG to discover if you have an abnormal thickening of the heart. This obstructs the flow of blood out of the heart, causing frequent and irregular heart rhythms that lead to sudden death." Dr. Thatcher paused for a moment to write some notes on his chart.

"I'm also going to have genetic testing performed to determine whether or not you have inherited one of the genes that causes HOCM. In addition to this, you'll undergo an exercise treadmill test to determine if exercise could provoke a dangerous heart rhythm."

Ryan nodded attentively. "OK. When are you going to schedule the testing?"

"There's no time like the present," Dr. Thatcher smiled at him. "I'd like to move on this right away."

Ryan nodded seriously but didn't say anything. His mind was trying hard to absorb all that was happening.

"There's a wheelchair waiting for you outside the door," Dr. Thatcher scribbled more notes on his chart. "I'll have Annie wheel you down to the fifth floor. Do you mind driving?" Dr Thatcher looked at Annie with a grin.

"I'd love to," Annie winked at Ryan.

"No speeding," the doctor warned jokingly.

"George," Annie smiled at the doctor playfully, "I'm not making any promises that I can't keep." Annie opened the door and rolled in the wheelchair.

"Can't I just walk?" Ryan protested the mode of transportation. "I feel stupid riding around the hospital in a wheelchair when I'm perfectly fine."

"Sorry Ryan," Dr. Thatcher spoke firmly, "it's hospital policy that you ride in the wheelchair." Then, turning toward Annie, the doctor whispered in a loud humorous voice, "You know, once we've got them in the wheelchair, it makes it much harder for them to escape!" Dr. Thatcher and Annie roared with laughter, while Ryan just sat there smirking at them.

"You're taxi, Sir." Annie waved a hand toward the wheelchair.

Ryan reluctantly got in and as soon as he did, Annie let out a low giggle. As she began pushing the wheelchair slowly down the hallway, she leaned close to Ryan's ear and whispered, "It's payback time!"

"You wouldn't take advantage of my pitiful situation." Instinctively, Ryan braced himself in the chair. The nightmarish ride to the hospital was still haunting him.

"Just watch me!" Annie's voice was low and serious. Ryan tensed up as a slow wave of panic washed over him. He knew he was at her mercy, and it was not a comfortable place to be.

Ryan turned his head so he could see Annie's face. "OK, like, what did I ever do to you? You're supposed to show compassion to people in the hospital, not torment them."

Annie put a hand on top of his head and turned it back around. Then, in her best airline attendant's voice, she stated, "Passengers will keep their heads forward and remain in an upright position." Annie laughed loudly and Ryan had to join her. This was the most fun he'd seen her have since they met.

Unfortunately, Ryan thought wearily, it was totally at his expense.

"And," as Annie took a corner a little too fast, "to answer your question, as to what you did to me, to deserve serious payback?" Ryan nodded, gripping the sides of the chair tightly. "Let's make a list, shall we?" Annie laughed again and Ryan simply shook his head and smiled.

"Do you recall," Annie asked doing her best Perry Mason voice, "someone stealing my picture and kidnapping me aboard their tour bus? Hum...does that ring any bells for you, Pal?"

"But you understand the reasons for that now, Annie," Ryan pleaded his case to her. "Surely, you're not going to hold that against me."

Annie stopped the wheelchair for a second and leaned close to his ear. "Watch me!"

Ryan slumped in his chair and grumbled teasingly, "You're too vengeful, Annie. It's not healthy for you."

Annie laughed and pulled the wheelchair to a stop again. She went around the chair and knelt down in front of it so she could look Ryan directly in the eye. "You're wrong," she added playfully, "I think revenge can be a wonderful way to get rid of stress! It can be very healthy!" Annie laughed as Ryan slumped deeper into his chair. "I'm just kidding-I'm not a vengeful type person. If I were,

I'd be looking for an isolated set of stairs to roll you down!" Annie could not contain her laughter.

"Stairs!" Ryan shouted, trying to get up out of the chair, "I don't care what hospital policy is, I'm walking!"

Annie lightheartedly put a hand to Ryan's chest and shoved him back in his chair. "But," she waved a stern finger in his face, "one thing that I'm not kidding about is practical jokes."

"Practical jo…" Ryan tried to say, suddenly appearing innocent and naïve.

Annie wasn't about to give him any leeway on this issue. "Yes." As she studied him intently, she went on. "My husband was a huge practical joker, and," Annie leaned in closer to him, "you have quite a reputation for them yourself."

"Who me?" Ryan was looking at her wide-eyed and way too innocently. It only confirmed his guilt. "I don't know how on earth you heard a thing like that."

So, Annie thought smiling coyly, he thinks he can pull one over on me. He's not even attempting a plea bargain. He's just totally denying what she knew was true. "Do you remember a concert you gave in New Hampshire?"

Ryan was trying so hard not to smile that his face looked strained. "Gee, New Hampshire? Great state, I've been there a lot." Then he turned and looked Annie right in the eye. "You're going to have to be a whole lot more specific than that if you're going to accuse me of something. Really, Annie...this is not a pretty side of you." He turned his head away, but not before Annie saw a slight smile start to creep up. That was all she needed.

"OK," Annie eyed him as she placed her hands on her hips, "how's this for specific. Do you remember being in New Hampshire, August 1999, at the Christian Music Festival at Loon Mountain?"

Ryan looked clearly surprised. "Wow, well now, that is pretty specific." Annie smiled broadly at him. "I was there...what's the charge, Counselor?"

Annie's smile grew even wider. "I suppose you want me to be specific on that too?"

Ryan actually smiled. "It would be helpful."

"OK, how's this for specific...Jay Thomas, who was your bass player at the time, and who by the way is another awful practical joker, had a birthday."

Ryan's eyebrows shot up. "You know, Annie, people have birthdays everyday. It's not an uncommon event."

"You made him a cake."

Ryan was grinning like a proud Cheshire cat. "Thoughtful of me, wasn't it?"

Annie laughed. "You are such a weasel. You're not going to admit it, are you?"

Ryan was still smiling victoriously at her. "What's there to admit? I made him a cake. I think you should be saying how thoughtful I was, instead of accusing me."

Annie laughed, leaned in, and placed the flat of her hand against his chest. "You didn't make him a cake, you turned him into a cake. You dumped flour, sugar, milk and eggs right over his head. I have several friends that were there and can corroborate my story word for word."

Ryan started to howl. "Hey, listen, there wasn't time to bake it. Ya know, it's really the thought that counts." His face went completely serious for a moment. "People so often forget that. It really cuts me so deeply."

They started laughing again. "You are such a comedian, Ryan. And, by the way, I know I've only hit the tip of the iceberg here with you're joking."

"That is so not true." He sighed deeply. "Ya know, you pull one little joke, and the world never forgets."

Annie laughed and a moment later Ryan did too. "Only one joke, huh? You sure you want to stick to that story. Remember, you are under oath here."

"Well, ya know," Ryan said a bit uneasily, "I didn't realize I was under oath here."

"So that makes it OK for you to lie?"

"Oh, lying under oath is definitely a whole lot worse than just plain lying. Hey, I've watched enough Perry Mason to know that. You never, ever lie under oath...especially," Ryan waved a finger at her, "if Perry Mason is cross examining you. That's very important."

"Thanks for the tip," Annie said insincerely, "but you still never answered the question."

"Hum, was there a question in there? I must have missed it."

"You're an awful practical joker. Admit it!"

"Hey, hey, hey," Ryan held both hands up in front of himself, "I am not an awful practical joker. Actually," the big grin was back on his face, "I'm quite good at them. A good practical joker doesn't get caught. And I," he announced proudly, "rarely get caught. I think it's a gift."

They both burst out laughing. "So how did you manage to get caught when you super soaked the Aussie band 'High Flyers'?"

Ryan looked at her and smirked. "Annie, sometimes you just have to take the dive. I mean, if you're going to super soak a band in front of ten thousand people, you're likely to get caught. You know, chances are one of them is going to tell on you."

Annie laughed. "You are awful, but you have just proven my point. I won this case. You're guilty and you're going to jail."

Ryan was clearly enjoying himself. "What? No chance for community service? You know, I can be a very good boy."

"Ryan, don't mess with me. I learned the craft from your brother. If you pull something on me, I guarantee you'll get it back in full force twice as bad."

Ryan was smiling again, his face filled with an impish expression. "This might be fun…"

"I don't want you to make me a cake."

"I'd only do that on your birthday," he said in a matter of fact way.

"Listen, I want to call a truce right now." Annie was completely serious. She knew this could quickly turn into a nightmare. "I want to be your friend, Ryan, not your great and worthy opponent."

Ryan nodded and smiled as he extended his hand toward her. "OK, let's shake on it."

As they shook hands, Ryan continued to hold hers a moment longer. "I want to thank you for everything that you're doing for me, Annie." His voice was sincere and loving. "You don't have to be here, but you are. That says a lot about who you are."

Annie smiled at him warmly and tried to ignore all the feelings racing through her at his very touch.

"Your brother would want me to do this." She gently pulled her hand back from his. As she went to the back of the wheelchair again, she spoke to him from her heart. "Besides, I want to be here for you. You're family."

"Thanks," Ryan was deeply moved. Family meant so much to him.

"Don't mention it," Annie squeezed his shoulder. "Now, let's go find some stairs!"

"Stairs!" Ryan bolted upright in his chair.

"I'm only kidding, brother-in-law." Annie chuckled to herself. "I never promised not to tease you. That would be too hard to resist!"

Six

Annie and Ryan listened carefully to Dr. Thatcher as he explained the results of the testing. "Mr. Jones," the doctor addressed him in a serious voice, "I have some good news for you and some bad news. What do you want to hear first?"

Ryan studied the doctor intently for a moment and then exhaled loudly. In an ultra calm voice, he asked to hear the good news first.

"Dr. Thatcher smiled slightly. "You're already in the hospital."

"That's the good news?" Ryan's voice had lost the ultra calm tone and had shot straight up to panic.

Dr. Thatcher slowly nodded. "Yes, Ryan. You're quite fortunate that you're here. You definitely have HOCM. You're one of the fortunate ones to have it diagnosed while you're still standing vertically."

"You're kidding!" Ryan gasped.

The doctor shook his head. "I'm afraid not. The good news is that we can successfully treat this condition. It is my professional opinion that we schedule surgery for tomorrow. I will insert an ICD, which is an internal defibrillator, through a small incision on the left side of your chest under the collarbone. The ICD wires are then passed through a vein and buried in the chest."

"OK," Ryan was very thoughtful; "I'd like to have a minute to discuss this with Annie."

When Dr. Thatcher left the room, Ryan looked over at Annie. Her eyes were full of tears and her face was as white as a sheet. Ryan walked over to her, feeling all choked up himself, and wrapped his arms tightly around her. They held each other for several minutes.

"Annie," Ryan whispered tenderly, pulling her back slightly to look into her tear stained face, "I don't know how to thank you."

Annie looked down at the floor, embarrassed by their intimacy. Ryan gently put a finger under her chin and slowly raised her head until their eyes met. His dark blue eyes were pooled in tears.

"Annie," Ryan's voice was filled with love, "you saved my life. Thank you doesn't even seem to come close to what it is I'm trying to say to you." Ryan bent down and brushed a soft kiss across Annie's cheek, and then held her tightly for a moment. Annie returned his hug, squeezing his big stocky frame.

It was at that moment that Dr. Thatcher walked back into the room. He stared at Annie and Ryan a moment before clearing his throat. Annie jumped away from Ryan quickly, as though she had been burned. Embarrassment flooded her face, while Ryan's face showed no regret about being caught in an intimate moment.

"I'm sorry to interrupt," Dr. Thatcher spoke apologetically, "but I do need to know if I should schedule surgery for tomorrow."

"Go ahead, Doc," Ryan said softly, but confidently. "But I don't understand," Ryan walked toward the doctor, "why you are waiting until tomorrow. I feel like a ticking time bomb waiting to explode."

"No need to worry," the doctor reassured, "You'll be fine. You'll be confined to your bed until morning. You won't get off your bed for any reason."

"Not even to go to the bathroom?" Ryan asked jokingly.

"No," the doctor smiled at him, "not even for that."

"Well," Ryan announced in an amused tone, "I'm not drinking anything until this is over. If I have to go, I'll just hold it and keep crossing my legs!"

Annie and Dr. Thatcher burst out laughing. "That's quite a plan you have there, Ryan, but I'm afraid that's not possible. You see, we'll have you hooked up to an I.V. and be pumping fluids into you. You're going to want to use the bathroom more than ever!"

Ryan looked at the doctor with a disappointed expression on his face. "Bed pan?" His eyes narrowed in disgust. The doctor nodded, and then left the room to make arrangements for the operation.

"We need to call my kids." Ryan's tone was urgent. "I want my girls to fly in from Chatfield Hollow."

"You're going to get your own room in a few minutes," Annie said quickly. "You'll have a phone in your room and you can call them from there. They can fly right into Boston, and I'll pick them up at Logan Airport. It's only a short ride from the hospital."

"Sounds like a good plan," Ryan smiled tenderly at her. "Thanks for taking such good care of me."

"Now stop that," Annie waved a hand toward him. "You have thanked me enough. I don't want to listen to you thanking me all night long."

Ryan laughed. "OK. OK."

When Ryan was settled in his room, he called his daughters, Beth and Nicole, who were both at school at Tennessee Christian College. He explained the situation to them, and asked them to take the first available flight to Boston. The girls called back within fifteen minutes saying they had a flight booked on United 1606 that was scheduled to arrive in Boston at 8:17 P.M.

"Good," Ryan nodded thoughtfully, "take a cab from the airport to Boston General. They've got me locked up here on the fifth floor."

After Ryan hung up the phone, he noticed Annie looking at him strangely. "What?"

"Ryan, I should be picking up your daughters from the airport."

Ryan shook his head emphatically. "Annie, I don't want you leaving me." He took her hand tenderly. "The best place for you right now is at my side. You can help keep me calm and keep my mind off this. Thanks for being here," he said in an emotional voice as he squeezed her hand tightly.

Annie slowly pulled her hand away from him and waved it directly in his face. "Just wait until you get my bill, Mister! Then you won't be so thankful!"

They laughed and then Annie phoned the house. She simply told Amy that their presence was requested here. She told her daughter that Ryan was going to be fine, but he would rather explain the situation in person.

When the crew from Annie's house arrived half an hour later, their faces registered shock as Ryan detailed the situation for them.

"Dad," David's voice was filled with sheer disbelief, "Annie was right!"

Ryan nodded seriously.

"Dad, she saved your life!" David broke down in tears while father and son hugged each other.

A few minutes later, David wiped away his tears and went to where Annie was standing. "Thank you," he squeaked out in a choked up voice. Then he threw his arms around her. "I'm so glad that God brought you into our lives, and I'm so glad that you pushed Dad into this."

Annie nodded and smiled. She felt too choked up to speak.

Soon after that, a nurse came into the room and ushered everyone out. "We need to get Mr. Jones settled and then you can come back in."

When Annie, David, Gil, and Amy returned to Ryan's room, they found him sitting up in bed, in a hospital gown, with a white bed sheet draped discreetly across his legs. Annie couldn't help but smile when she saw him.

"Yeah, yeah," Ryan pretended to be disgusted, "they got me back in this dress again. Go ahead and laugh. I know you're just dying to!" Everyone did laugh, but not because he was wearing the gown again, but because he was just so funny about it.

Later that evening, Ryan's girls arrived from Chatfield Hollow and the family reunion continued.

After Ryan explained to his daughter how he and Annie met, about the picture, the bus ride, his brother…his oldest daughter eyed him carefully.

"Dad," Beth couldn't hide the amusement in her voice, "you are lucky that your hunches about the picture were right. If Annie didn't turn out to be your brother's wife, you'd probably be sitting in the police station right now instead of in a hospital."

Ryan laughed loudly. "That's true, Beth, but Annie did get her revenge." Annie smiled widely. "Don't ever let her take you for a ride in a wheelchair!" Ryan's voice was full of mischief and humor.

Everyone looked at Ryan with a puzzled expression, except for Annie who was quietly laughing. Ryan went on to explain "the ride" that Annie had given him, and the room broke out laughing.

"Sounds like you got off easy, Dad." Ryan looked over curiously at his middle child Nicole. With an impish look in her eyes, she turned and asked Annie, "Do you want me to help you find a long, lonely set of stairs?"

"Hey!" Ryan spoke up quickly, "Whose side are you on anyway?"

"Dad," Beth sat down on his bed, "at this moment, we're all on Annie's side. You're lucky she didn't pop you in the nose."

"You're right," Ryan touched his nose for a minute, "she is a bit feisty!"

The conversation was quick and fun-spirited for the next several hours. At eleven o'clock, the bouncer nurse told Ryan that everyone had to leave. "You need a good night's rest, Mr. Jones."

Ryan complained immediately. "I'm not going to sleep anyway. I just know it. Having my family around will help keep my mind off the surgery."

Bouncer studied Ryan carefully. "OK," she sounded like an Army General, "everyone goes but your wife. The rest of the clan can come back tomorrow morning and see you before surgery." With her orders given, Bouncer left the room. Things grew very, very quiet.

A nervous laugh escaped Annie's lips and everyone else joined in. "Now where in the world would she ever get an idea like that?"

"Well," David quickly volunteered, "you are the right age." A mischievous smile was plastered across the young teen's face. Everyone laughed.

"Listen, you three," Annie addressed Ryan's kids, "I am your aunt. Remember that!" The group ignored her firm tone and started laughing again. Annie had to smile. They were a silly bunch and it was hard not to join in.

"So, Annie," Beth asked seriously, "are you going to stay with Dad?"

Annie couldn't hide her surprise. She glanced over at Ryan, and he smiled at her invitingly. "You're the best choice here, Annie. I could never choose between one of my kids, and Gil already sees too much of me."

Gil laughed quietly and nodded in agreement. "That's true."

"This way," Ryan continued, "you can tell me stories about my brother and keep my mind off tomorrow morning's surgery."

Annie looked over at Ryan's kids, and they all urged her to stay. She nodded in agreement. She was more than glad to stay with Ryan, especially at a time like this. The last few days had been some of the happiest of her life since her husband's death. She did want to get to know her husband's brother better. Husband's brother...Annie thought closing her eyes for a moment. Yes, he was that, but Annie could no longer successfully deny that he was quickly becoming something more. Quietly she prayed and asked the Lord for wisdom and guidance. This situation was becoming increasingly confusing. Yet, she thought smiling at Ryan, it was also becoming more interesting by the minute.

Seven

As Annie made herself comfortable in the blue, vinyl chair that a nurse had rolled in the room for her, Ryan watched her, with just a hint of a grin playing around the corners of his mouth. Annie studied him for a moment, and she instantly saw that his eyes were dancing with amusement. She knew something was definitely up. "What?" she asked him shyly, suddenly feeling very self-conscious.

Ryan laughed quietly. "I'm waiting to hear the story of your life."

Annie looked at him with a startled expression on her face. Then, narrowing her eyes slightly, she said in a direct voice, "I thought we agreed that you wouldn't ask me personal questions. She raised an eyebrow at him suspiciously. Annie found that her heart and her head were in a die-hard battle with her feelings toward Ryan Jones. Right now, unfortunately for Ryan, the head was winning the battle, and she didn't feel like discussing anything personal with him at all.

Ryan laughed loudly this time. Then he shrugged his shoulders and spread his arms open wide. "Annie, I'm your brother-in-law. I would have heard all the stories before by now anyway. You'd just be bringing me up-to-date a little. Besides," he paused to look down at his blue hospital gown a minute, "I'm sitting here in a hospital dress, without much underneath, waiting for surgery tomorrow." Ryan looked at her with a friendly grin. "We've gone way beyond that 'No Trespassing' sign that you hold out to strangers."

Annie laughed nervously. The man was able to read her mind with amazing accuracy. It was completely unnerving. "No Trespassing sign?" Annie echoed back at him, trying to sound like she hadn't the faintest idea what he was talking about.

"Yeah," Ryan smiled obnoxiously, "you have a sense about yourself that makes it clear to others that you aren't inviting them to ask you any personal questions." He paused and laughed again. "Like I said before, we're way beyond that point."

Annie nodded and smiled. She felt convicted about her hot and cold attitude toward him. She didn't mean to act that way; she was just scared of the emotions he brought out in her. He wasn't content to stay on the surface. He opened himself up and had a way of opening her up that she wasn't quite sure she was ready for. Annie looked at him and tried to smile but couldn't. "You're right, I'm sorry. It's just that you scare me sometimes. I don't think I'm ready for you." The words were spoken quieter than a whisper, but Ryan caught each one and the emotional anguish with which they were spoken.

"You don't need to be afraid of me." His words were honest and sincere. "I won't hurt you." Annie stared at him a moment. A slight nod of her head told him that she had heard him and the scared look in her eyes told him she didn't quite believe him. He felt she wanted to, but he also knew any kind of relationship with Annie needed a lot of prayer and a lot of time. Speaking of time, he also knew it was time to change the subject.

As Ryan took a sip from his water cup, he glanced down at his hospital gown and knew it was the perfect conversation piece. It was obvious to anyone who came in the room that he was not happy wearing it. He looked over at Annie seriously. "Don't you think this looks a little feminine? I wonder if they gave me a girl's dress instead of a boy's dress?"

Annie laughed loudly, and Ryan smiled at her. "Ryan, first of all it's a hospital gown not a dress. All the patients have to wear them. Secondly, there is only one style of hospital gown for everybody. It's not male or female; it's unisex."

"Yeah," he was studying his gown closely, "but look at these little blue flowers." He looked at her and then pointed to the pattern. "Guys don't wear little blue flowers like this." His words were spoken firm and adamantly.

Annie felt herself relaxing as she laughed again at Ryan. This was going to be a fun night. She paused to take a sip of tea that Bouncer had brought in for her. "They're not flowers, they're little starbursts. Now stop worrying. I couldn't find my video recorder, so, no one will ever know. Which by the way is really too bad," she smiled mischievously at him, "because I'm sure this is just the type of thing that the tabloid papers would eat up. You know, all those inquiring minds…"

Ryan glared at her, and she just continued to smile. A sudden thought jarred Annie's mind and she jumped up and walked across the room to where her pocketbook lay. As she rummaged through it, Ryan asked her in a curious tone what she was looking for.

"I think I have one of those little disposable cameras in here. We might be able to get a shot of you after all."

Ryan started to struggle with his sheets as if he were going to try to get out of bed.

"Hey! Hey!" Annie's tone was disapproving as she jabbed a finger toward him, "You're not allowed out of bed." They looked fiercely at each other for a moment, before Ryan reluctantly sank back against the headboard of his bed.

Annie went back to rummaging through her pocketbook. "Oh, here it is!" Annie held up a small, yellow, disposable camera. "Look what I found." She waved it in his direction victoriously.

"You're not going to use that!" Ryan was emphatic.

"Yes," Annie answered him impishly, "I am!"

As she walked closer to his bed, zooming the camera in on him, he protested vehemently. "This is nothing short of blackmail! You're taking advantage of my helpless situation."

"Yes," Annie replied grinning at him, "I am. Now, if you want to offer me a fair price, before I go to the tabloid papers, mind you, I'm not greedy. I'm a reasonable businesswoman and absolutely willing to listen to any offer that you might be prepared to make."

Annie snapped a quick shot of an unsmiling Ryan Jones just as Nurse Bouncer walked through the door. "Here," she took the camera from Annie hands, "let me take a picture of the two of you."

Annie began to back away. She didn't mind performing the service for others, but she absolutely hated having her picture taken. "No, no," the words quickly flew out of her mouth, "that's OK. I just wanted a shot of the patient. You know, something for his scrapbook."

"Come on, Annie," Ryan was smiling and his tone was teasing. "Come over here and sit next to me." He was tossing her an absolutely charming smile in an attempt to reel her into the picture. "If I have to suffer," Ryan threw a hand across his chest dramatically, "then so do you."

Annie started to protest again, but Bouncer gave her an encouraging nudge toward the bed that almost knocked her over. Annie quickly regained her balance, but not before her ears heard Ryan's muffled snickers. She targeted him with her eyes and he burst out laughing.

She knew there was no easy way out of this, so she went to the edge of Ryan's bed, ready to endure the stupid picture. "My, how the tables have turned." Ryan laughed loudly again. "I'm so glad that you could be a part of this." Annie couldn't help but laugh. She had tried to throw a pie in his face, but instead, wound up getting it back in her own face at full force.

"Annie," Bouncer barked in a movie director's tone, "you're going to have to move in closer to Ryan. I can't get you both in the picture."

Getting closer to Ryan was exactly what her head told her not to do. If anything, she felt like she needed to get away from this man before she was completely, hopelessly smitten. As Annie stared at Ryan Jones for a second, it suddenly struck her that even the North Pole would not be far enough away.

Ryan simply smiled at the intense expression on Annie's face. "I don't bite," he hummed softly.

That broke the ice and Annie soon found herself smiling and pushing herself up against the side of Ryan's shoulder. Bouncer gave them a few more commanding instructions and just before she snapped the picture, she said in a cheery tone, "It's always so nice to have a husband and wife picture."

Annie and Ryan smiled ear to ear at the comment.

"Oh, that was a great shot!" Bouncer proclaimed enthusiastically as she handed the camera back to Annie. "Really great shot," she mumbled as she went to check Ryan's I.V. line and took his blood pressure and temperature.

After Bouncer left the room, Annie turned to Ryan with an embarrassed smile on her face. "We really should tell her, ya know?"

Ryan laughed and Annie could tell that he was enjoying the charade. "Nah...let her think what she wants. Besides," Ryan became very serious, "if she finds out you're not my wife, she may throw you out on the street. She's a tough old general and I don't want to be alone tonight."

Annie nodded understandingly. Even through all his humor and politeness, Annie could tell that Ryan was working hard to be brave. Heart surgery was no small matter and she felt she had to do her best to keep his mind off it.

Annie touched his arm gently as she snuggled back into her recliner. "How about a story?"

"A story?" Ryan's face lit up. "I love stories!"

Annie smiled. "I thought this would be a good time to tell you part B of my life story."

"Part B?" Ryan was clearly dissatisfied. "What about part A? I don't want to miss a thing."

"Oh, we might get to that sometime later," Annie waved a hand at him passively. "Part B is much better. That's about the time that I first met your brother."

"Oh, a romantic story," Ryan winked at Annie. "I love romantic stories."

"Just remember," Annie waved a finger at him, "I expect to hear the story on you and Kay sometime soon."

"No problem. It's a story that I love to tell."

Annie nodded and then settled back into her recliner. A loving smile spread across her face as she remembered the first time she had met Ryan Smith. "I will never forget the first time that I saw him." Annie smiled down into her teacup. "I was sixteen and my girlfriend Alex and I had been out mopeding for the day." Annie glanced over at Ryan. "That's what we did growing up. Most of us were too poor to afford our own cars, so we had mopeds."

He nodded and she smiled at him and then continued. "It was about five o'clock and we were heading back to Alex's house for dinner. Her house was located on one of the steepest hills around, so as the mopeds began to climb it, they slowed down to about two miles an hour." Annie laughed, remembering it. "Mopeds don't like hills unless they're going down them. Sometimes, we'd actually get off the bikes and push them up the hill."

Ryan laughed. "Yeah, I'm familiar with the gutless bikes."

Annie smiled. "So, there we were, putting up this steep hill, when all of a sudden, I spotted a black, 1965 Shelby Mustang coming toward us. It was a GT350, complete with wide racing stripes." Annie closed her eyes a moment. "I love fast cars."

Ryan smiled warmly. "So do I."

"Anyway, I said Alex, 'look at that car! That is so cool!' Well, as her head popped up from staring at her speedometer, she said excitedly, 'Oh, that's Ryan Smith. You've got to meet him. He's Paul's best friend." Annie paused for a minute. "By the way, Paul was Alex's tennis partner."

"I'm with you," Ryan winked at her.

"Well, when Alex talked about meeting Ryan I panicked. One rule my father had about riding the moped was that you had to wear a motorcycle helmet. The thing was as ugly as could be. It was shiny white and looked like a great big egg. I grabbed my friend's arm and told her I didn't want to meet him. There was no way I'd want to meet any guy wearing that helmet. I felt so stupid and looked like an egghead."

Ryan laughed loudly at this. "An egghead, huh?"

Annie nodded. "Yes," she laughed quietly. She stopped to take a sip of her tea.

"So," Ryan had a huge smirk on his face, "I bet she introduced you to Ryan Smith anyway."

"She did!" Annie answered a little angrily. "I was so mad at her. You know," Annie laughed, "I was going through my delicate, sensitive teenage years. Things like this could wipe you out for a while."

Ryan laughed. "Yeah, but you got over it."

Annie smiled and nodded. "Anyway, when this hot Mustang pulled over to us, my friend quickly made the introductions and then talked with Ryan for several minutes. The first time I looked at his face..." Annie smiled shyly, "I swear my heart stopped beating. I mean," she glanced over at

Ryan, "it was like I was frozen in place. I couldn't move, talk, breathe or think."

"Love at first sight." Ryan sighed loudly.

"Yes," Annie nodded thoughtfully. "It was, at least for me...and then he drove off." Annie laughed softly. "You know," she stared off distantly for a moment, "Ryan was the only guy that ever had that effect on me. I never fell for any guy the way I fell for him."

Annie glanced at Ryan awkwardly and mumbled apprehensively, "I don't usually tell people that."

"Annie," Ryan assured her lovingly, "we're family. Your secrets are safe with me."

Annie nodded shyly.

"So, what happened next?" Ryan asked interestedly.

Annie smiled. "Well, after I got over my initial heart attack, I started pumping my friend for all the info she had on Ryan Smith. And," Annie shook her head, "the first thing she told me made my heart drop."

"He had a girlfriend?" Ryan guessed quickly.

"No," Annie smiled at him, "he was in college."

"So?" Ryan asked, obviously not understanding the connection.

"Ryan, I was a sixteen-year-old sophomore in high school. I had just been given the green light to start dating by my parents. If I had brought Ryan

Smith home, my father would have chased him off with a gun!"

Ryan laughed. "Really? Your dad was that protective of you?"

Annie shook her head and then asked in an amused voice, "What would you do if your sweet sixteen-year-old daughter brought home a college boy on her first date?" Annie studied Ryan and watched as his face grew serious.

"I wouldn't have run him off with a gun, I'd have shot him with it so he couldn't come back and bother my daughter!"

Annie laughed. "Now you're talking like a father that adores his little girl."

"So, was that the end of it?"

"For a while…" Annie slowly admitted. "Though, you know, I never quite could get him out of my mind. Every time I saw his Mustang around town, I went into a quiet, but full-fledged heart attack. What an awful time that was."

"Anyway, about a year later, my friend invited me to a tennis tournament that she and her partner Paul were playing in. When I arrived at the courts, I saw Ryan Smith sitting next to my friend's mother. The mother saw me, and waved me over, and I took a seat next to her. As she went to introduce us, I stuttered out nervously, "Oh, we've already met." Ryan looked over at me, with a curious expression on his face, and I knew I'd just made a serious mistake."

Ryan howled with laughter. "Yeah, because now you had to explain the egg head thing. Am I right?"

Annie laughed. "That's exactly right! I was mortified. It was the most embarrassing situation of my young life. After I explained when we had met, Ryan Smith said, "Oh yeah, you were the girl in the white motorcycle helmet. I didn't recognize you without your helmet."

"Well," Annie rolled her eyes at Ryan, "that's not exactly what a girl dreams of hearing! After that brief conversation, Ryan turned his attention back to the game. I was simply crushed. I wanted to walk off the court that instant, but I knew if I did, I'd only draw attention to myself."

"So, I take it that's not when you and my brother hit it off."

Annie laughed loudly as Ryan gazed at her sympathetically. "Don't you dare feel sorry for me. Please. It all worked out in the end. God's timing was perfect."

Ryan nodded understandingly, and Annie continued. "Throughout the next year, I dated many guys. I never dated seriously, only casually. I wasn't looking for a serious relationship, only a fun companion."

"So, you were a big flirt!"

Annie laughed. "I guess, in a way. But, I knew that if I dated the same guy too many times, he'd think I was serious about him and I didn't want to hurt anyone."

"That was very considerate of you," Ryan murmured sarcastically.

Annie ignored him and continued on. "Anyway, about a year later, the fall of my senior year, I met Ryan Smith again. This time," Annie purred excitedly, "it was different."

"Wedding bells were ringing!"

Annie laughed. "No, silly, he not only remembered me but he talked to me like a regular person. We were in my friend's church and Ryan came over and sat next to me. Before the service started, we talked with each other easily. I could see the interest in his big blue eyes, and, he was actually flirting with me!"

"So, what happened?"

"My brand new boyfriend came over and sat down on the other side of me!" Annie couldn't contain her laughter.

"That sounds just a bit awkward."

"It was!" Annie laughed remembering it. "It was the longest church service of my entire life!"

"I'll bet," Ryan laughed. "Better you than me!"

Annie ran a hand through her short brown hair. "Let's see, I guess it was about two months later that I saw Ryan."

"Now, the big fireworks. Am I right?"

"Nope."

"You still had a boyfriend?"

"No, I had broken it off with him, but, Ryan had a girlfriend! Can you believe it?"

They both laughed loudly. "I'm sure she was a bimbo!" Ryan teased.

"Completely!" Annie quickly agreed. A moment later her face grew thoughtful. "You know, as much as I hate to admit it, she was a good looking, popular, Christian girl. She was really very nice."

"That's nice of you to admit." Ryan winked at her.

"Hey, it's easy to admit it now. That was all a long time ago. Besides," Annie smiled triumphantly at him, "I married Ryan!"

"It's amazing that you two ever got together."

"I know," Annie agreed quickly. "God definitely wanted us together and didn't give up on us."

"So, what happened next?"

"Next, hum, let's see. Oh! You're going to love this!" Annie laughed. "That spring, still my senior year in high school, Ryan and I met again. I can't believe this happened," Annie smiled at the memory. "Ryan stopped by to visit my girlfriend's father. Her father was very good at electrical things and Ryan needed some help with something. Anyway, when Ryan was heading out the door, my friend asked him if he wanted to go see a Christian movie called, A Thief In The Night. He said sure, and my friend said good, you can pick Annie up at seven. She gave him directions to my house and that was that!"

"Ryan accepted the situation?"

Annie nodded. "So, my matchmaker friend calls me and asks me the same question. How would I like to see a movie? When I said sure, she said that Ryan Smith was going to pick me up at seven and then she hung up the phone! I was completely hysterical! I tried to call her back but the little imp took the phone off the hook! Can you believe it? I looked at my watch and almost fainted when I realized that I had only fifteen minutes to get ready before Ryan would be at my house. I could have killed my friend!"

Ryan laughed. "It sounds like something you might do!" Ryan smiled and then winked at Annie. He was having a great time.

Annie just smiled at him smugly. "Anyway, later Ryan told me that when he got to the end of the road, he panicked when he saw two red houses. My girlfriend had told him to go to the red house at the end of North Road. But," Annie paused dramatically throwing her hands in the air, "when he got to the end of North Road, there were two red houses, one on the left and one on the right."

"You're kidding!" Ryan sat up a little straighter in bed.

"No," Annie smiled at him, "there were two red houses at the end of the road and they sat exactly opposite each other!"

"What did he do?"

"When he looked in our driveway, he saw my dad's car and it had a Christian bumper sticker on it. I forget what it said, but anyway, it gave Ryan an idea of where to start."

"He could have just asked your neighbor where you lived."

"Oh! This story just keeps getting better! I forgot to tell you this. Ryan couldn't remember my name! He felt so nervous about picking me up that he couldn't remember my name!"

Ryan Jones's mouth dropped open and he stared at Annie in disbelief. "I think you're making this all up."

Annie laughed. "I'm not making it up. I promise you, it's all too true and that's why it's so funny! Can you imagine it? The man of my dreams can't even remember my name."

"It was probably nerves, Annie. I'm a wreck myself from listening to this story."

Annie laughed. "I know it was. My dad said that Ryan was practically shaking when he answered the door."

"Your dad answered the door?"

Annie smiled. "That was his policy. He always answered the door to check out my gentleman callers."

"What did Ryan say to him since he couldn't even remember your name?"

"My dad knew who Ryan was. Dad invited him in and told him that Annie would be ready in a minute."

"So, your dad helped him with the name thing." Ryan smiled. "That was nice."

"Yeah, dad has a kind heart. Besides, he loved Ryan's Mustang. Do you know that later, when I actually started dating Ryan, my dad accused me of dating Ryan just because I loved his car?"

"Really?"

"Yeah," Annie nodded and smiled, "but I knew that dad was only joking. He knew me better than that."

"So," Ryan asked pointedly, "you weren't the type of girl to date a guy only for his car."

"No way!" Annie replied quickly. "I had high Christian standards that didn't include dating a guy for what he drove, what he looked like, or what he did." Annie paused and looked at Ryan seriously.

"I strictly went for the heart. If a guy had a good, kind, sensitive, godly heart...I might consider dating him."

"Consider him?" Ryan raised an eyebrow at Annie, "You sound like you're buying a cow!"

Annie laughed. "Ryan, you know me better than that!"

He playfully winked at her.

"Just because a guy has a godly heart doesn't mean that he's the right one for me to date. There has to be a certain chemistry and compatibility."

Ryan winked again. "You bet!" He grinned flirtatiously. "So, you went to the movie."

Annie nodded. "Yeah, I finally got a ride in the dream machine."

"How romantic. You're finally going out with the guy of your dreams, in the car of your dreams."

"Well, not exactly." Annie chewed on her bottom lip for a moment. "My parents were crammed into the back seat of the Mustang."

"Your parents chaperoned you?"

"Well, in an indirect way. You see, they were going to the same movie we were, and my dad, being the practical Yankee that he is, strongly suggested to Ryan that we all ride together. So," shrugged her shoulders, "we did!"

"Boy, doesn't that just sound cozy," Ryan moaned sarcastically as he ran a hand through his thick brown hair.

"Not really," Annie rolled her eyes at him. "Anyway, the four of us went to the movies."

"And, Ryan asked you out! Am I right?"

Annie laughed. "No...I think he was planning to, but an old, pain in the neck boyfriend showed up at the movie, too. He pestered me throughout the entire movie, and even more afterwards. I was on the verge of tears by the time I got home."

"That's generally not the best time to ask a young lady out on a date."

Annie laughed. "That's true! Well, the next day Ryan called me and finally, after three and a half years of dreaming, he asked me out on a date!"

"Ta-da!" Ryan clapped his hands. "Then you two hit it off and lived happily ever after. Right?"

"Wrong," Annie shook her head. "He asked me out, but I couldn't go. I was leaving to be a camp counselor for the next month. I told Ryan I'd call him when I got back from camp."

"Oh, man," Ryan threw his hands in the air, "you're killing me, Annie. Your story is slowly killing me."

"Do you want me to stop?"

"No," Ryan answered quickly.

"It's getting late," Annie studied the big clock on the wall. "It's already 1:30."

"Please," Ryan begged, "you've got to continue to the part where you two start dating. I won't be able to fall asleep if you don't. I'll be up the rest of the night wondering how on earth you two finally got together."

"OK. OK. "Annie mumbled as a big yawn escaped her mouth. "I forgot where I was."

"Camp," Ryan quickly pointed out. "You were about to go off to camp for a month."

"Oh yeah," Annie smiled at him sleepily. "Camp. Well, I went to camp, and, to make a long story short, I fell for a tall, handsome, dark-haired, blue-eyed piano player. He was an incredible musician, and" Annie wiggled her eyebrows at him, "as charming as they come. He quickly swept me off my feet."

"You have got to be kidding!" Ryan appeared shocked and disgusted. "You," he threw and accusing finger in her direction, "were supposed to be saving your heart for my brother."

Annie had to laugh at him. "Listen, Ryan, your brother and I weren't even dating yet. We weren't even good friends. You act as though I were cheating on him. I really didn't even know him yet."

"I'm sorry, Annie. I'm just anxious for the two of you to get together, that's all." He paused for a minute, and looked at her with a mischievous twinkle brewing in his deep blue eyes. "So, you fell for a dark-haired, blue-eyed, piano playing charmer, huh?"

Annie just giggled.

"You know," he narrowed his eyes at her, "you seem to have quite a pattern here for falling for dark-haired, blue-eyed musicians."

"I know it," Annie shot back in a spunky tone. "It's a bad habit, and I'm trying my best to break it!"

Ryan pretended to be shocked. "So, what happened to the bum?"

"Well, basically after camp, I headed off for my freshman year of college. I had to get there early because I was on the volleyball team. The piano player and I wrote for a month or so before I smartened up to the ways of long distance relationships."

Ryan nodded understandingly. "I think I know what you're getting at. People certainly can be different in letters than they are in person. Sometimes the view from a distance is not the same one you get up close."

"You got that right!"

"So, what happened to my brother during this time?"

"Well, this is an interesting part," Annie replied slowly with a puzzled look on her face. "Remember how I told him I would call him when I got back from camp?"

Ryan nodded expectantly.

"I feel like the Lord must have blocked it from my mind because I completely forgot."

"You stood my brother up?" Ryan shouted in disbelief.

"Calm down, mighty avenger," Annie teased. "Once you get to know me more, you will see that I am a person that is very loyal to my word. If I make a promise, I always, always follow through."

"Even if you decided that you didn't like the guy anymore?" Ryan was clearly skeptical.

"Yes, Ryan, even if I decided I didn't care for the guy." Annie stared at Ryan for a moment, a little annoyed by his attitude. "At the very least, I would have called him, like I said I would have, and told him I wasn't interested. Actually," Annie ran a hand through her hair, "I had planned to invite Ryan over for Sunday dinner. Our Sunday dinners always included a bunch of interesting people from church. The conversations were lively and fun, and I knew Ryan would have had a good time." Annie looked over at her patient again. "I am a very loyal person, Ryan."

Ryan nodded and touched her hand. "I know that you are Annie. You put up with me wonderfully these past few days."

"I know," Annie glared at him seriously, "it's my penance!"

"Penance!" Ryan said half joking and half shocked. "I hope I haven't been that bad."

Annie laughed in spite of her effort to try to keep a straight face. "I'm only kidding…"She touched his arm for a second. "You've been great, and, its been fun…and interesting, getting to know you. Never a dull moment."

They both laughed. "So, where are we now?" Ryan asked gazing at her through sleepy eyes.

"We're at 2:15, and I think we should get some rest." Annie gently tugged on the pillow beneath her head.

"No, No!" Ryan quickly objected. "You promised me you'd get to the part where you two started dating. And," Ryan wiggled a finger at her, "as you stated earlier, you are a person that's true to her word."

Annie laughed. She was really feeling very comfortable around Ryan Jones now and enjoying his company a great deal. "OK," Annie tried to suppress her smile, "we eventually started dating, got married and had two wonderful kids. That about sums it up." Annie rolled over and pretended to fall asleep in her recliner.

A moment later, a finger poked her in the ribs, and she practically flew out of her chair. "Hey!" she eyed him suspiciously, "Don't do anything to me that you don't want coming back at you!"

Ryan's grin spread across his face so slowly and seductively that Annie gasped. All of a sudden, she realized how he had taken her comment. "I didn't mean what you're thinking." As she straightened herself in her chair, she menacingly narrowed her eyes at him. "Where is your mind?"

Ryan's smile only widened and his blue eyes twinkled like fireworks going off.

"Now stop that!" Annie was feeling uncomfortable with her brother-in-law's flirting.

"I'm only smiling at what you said," Ryan claimed innocently.

"No," Annie waved a finger at him sternly, "you're smiling at an incorrect interpretation of what I said."

Ryan continued to smile wickedly. He simply had no shame.

"I meant," Annie turned away from his steady gaze, "that if you tickle me, or poke me, you're likely to end up with a bucket of ice down that dress that you're wearing."

Ryan seemed more amused then ever. "Dress? I knew it was a dress all along. I want you to know that you never had me fooled about it."

" I meant to say gown. Honest. It was just a little Freudian slip. Listen, I think you should close those dancing eyes of yours and go to sleep."

"I'm not tired," Ryan sounded like a little kid that didn't want to go to bed. "Besides, you have to finish your story."

Annie looked over at Ryan and felt intimidated by the way he zoomed in on her. The man was a hawkeye and didn't miss a thing. His radar was locked on her and wasn't about to change anytime too soon. "Well," Annie said slowly but determinedly, "if I'm going to finish my story, you're going to have to wipe that annoying smirk off your face."

"Done." Ryan masked his emotions under a blank expression.

"I keep forgetting where I left off," Annie mumbled, slightly disarmed by the blank expression covering Ryan's face. Only his eyes held a hint of humor. This expression was actually worse than the other one. He was trying to fool her, but he wasn't at all.

"I believe you are one month into your freshman year of college."

"Boy, are you paying attention," Annie eyed him carefully. "Too much attention," she mumbled under her breath.

Ryan just nodded and smiled.

"OK, college…about mid fall I met Kevin."

"Was he another dark-haired, blue-eyed musician?"

"How did you guess?"

"How long did that last?" Ryan's curiosity was apparent.

"A few months," Annie rolled her eyes at him. "When I brought him home over the break, his true colors broke loose. He was self-centered, obnoxious, and even my easy going dad asked me when he was going to leave."

"He must have been pretty bad."

"I could kick myself for dating him now. The fun side of him was fun until I realized that the guy could never hold a serious conversation. When he came to visit during break, it finally hit me that this character was never going to grow up."

Ryan nodded. "Yeah, I've met people like that."

"Anyway, in January when I returned to school, I was injured in a basketball game. I broke my ankle and had to have surgery and pins to repair it." Annie glanced down at her ankle for a moment.

"How's it now?" Ryan asked in a concerned voice.

"Fine. Thanks." It wasn't something that she liked to talk about. "I missed the spring semester of college because of my ankle. Ryan heard about it and called me."

"So, this is it. Right?"

"No," Annie laughed. "When he called, my mom and dad had just gotten me situated, cast and all in our car. I was on the way to the doctor's." Annie paused reflectively. "When dad came out to the car, he told me that some guy was on the phone for me. I was sure it was Kevin."

"The clown from college?"

"Yeah, the clown from college," Annie laughed at Ryan's description of Kevin. "He was convinced that we belonged together and told me that God told him that we should get married!" Annie burst out laughing. "Can you believe that?"

"Interesting proposal." Ryan winked at her. "What did you say?"

Annie laughed. "At first I was too surprised to speak. Then, after the initial shock wore off, I felt steamed. I felt like, how dare he use the Lord's name for his own personal advantage. Then," Annie smiled widely, "I counted to ten- twice! I knew I needed some time to cool down. I was mad enough that what I would have said to him would have definitely not been lady-like or Christian. It really wasn't a priority at that point. I've never been one to take being manipulated well. Guess I'm kind of picky, but it basically ticks me off when I think I'm being used. So, I counted to ten again to give myself time to change perspective and was able to pray a quick 911 prayer to ask for God's help." Annie laughed. "You know, it's a good thing that God doesn't answer all our prayers our way, because I vaguely remember something about lightning bolts, fire and hailstone in that prayer. I was kind of mad."

"Understandably so." Ryan had another one of those annoying smirks growing across his face. "So, when you finally spoke to this lying, little snake, what did you say?"

Annie smiled. "I firmly told him that God did not tell me that, and, in no way was I even remotely interested in him at all."

"Wow, that must have taken care of the weasel."

"Not really," Annie admitted slowly, "but I'll save that for another time. Remember the phone call?" Ryan nodded. "Well, it wasn't Kevin on the phone; it was Ryan. My dad told him to call back in five minutes, and when he did, no one answered the phone because we had left for the doctor's office."

"That's awful!" Ryan stared at Annie in disbelief.

"I know. Isn't it?" Annie laughed quietly. "My dad is very absent minded at times. We used to tease him and tell him he should wear a 'Hello, my name is' sticker on his shirt so he wouldn't forget his own name. He just told me that he told the guy to call back." Annie shook her head and laughed again. "I just assumed it was Kevin and forgot about it."

"I bet Ryan didn't forget about it."

"You're right! He didn't!" Annie smiled. "About a month later, my best friend called me and asked me if I wanted to go to the mall with her. Even though I was still on crutches and had just had my cast removed, I was stir-crazy and dying to get out."

Ryan nodded understandingly. "I know the feeling."

"When I drove up to her house, I was surprised to see Ryan's Mustang in her driveway. As I hobbled into the house, Ryan was sitting on the couch talking to my friend's boyfriend. As soon as he saw me, his eyes filled with fire. I was shocked and surprised until he starting speaking."

"The phone call..." Ryan guessed.

"That's right," Annie nodded her head. "He said in a low angry voice from across the room, "Why didn't you answer your phone last month?"

"I stared at him, feeling completely confused, when suddenly I remembered the call. The pieces fell together for me pretty quickly after that."

"I wish I could have been there," Ryan smiled impishly at her. "That whole fly on the wall thing is very appealing at times."

Annie laughed. "Yeah, well, I can tell you that my best friend was having the time of her life. A real live drama playing out right in her living room."

"So," Ryan asked curiously, "what did you do? Run to him and beg for his forgiveness?"

"Uh, no. I kind of started laughing."

"Laughing?" Ryan was clearly confused.

"Yes, laughing," Annie looked at him with a big grin. "I wasn't being mean or anything. I was just so surprised to find out it was Ryan on the phone that day. I couldn't believe we kept missing each other all these years. All the things that kept us apart-by now the list had really added up."

"Sounds like a poor excuse for laughing at my brother," Ryan tried to act defensive.

"Just listen to the rest," Annie touched his shoulder lightly. "I hobbled across the room on my crutches and told Ryan that we really needed to talk. We went outside, sat on the porch swing, and straightened the whole mess out in a few minutes."

"Clear, honest, communication is important."

"That's right!" Annie agreed, smiling back at him. "So, my girlfriend, her boyfriend, and Ryan and I went to the mall for the afternoon. Ryan and

I had a great time. We talked non-stop the entire afternoon. And then, that night, as I was getting into my car to leave, Ryan asked me out on a date!"

"Finally!" Ryan announced triumphantly. "And you said yes and went out with him." Ryan's eyes narrowed momentarily and skepticism had crept into his voice. "You did go out with him, didn't you?"

"Pretty much," Annie replied casually.

"Pretty much?" Ryan targeted her with his eyes, "And just what does that mean?"

"Well," a mischievous smile spread across Annie's face, "you know how I can get giddy when I'm tired?"

"First hand," Ryan answered quickly.

"He asked me out for Friday night, and I honestly couldn't go. I had promised to do something with my mom. As soon as I said I couldn't, Ryan quickly, almost urgently asked me out for Saturday night."

"I don't like the sound of this," Ryan's voice was stern. "I just know this is not going to a good place." He stared at her for a second, and then said slowly, "You did say yes, didn't you?"

"Not exactly...you see, he had such a determined expression on his face, that I couldn't seem to help myself. A horrible thought crossed my mind. I wondered how many times he would keep asking me out."

Ryan's mouth dropped open but no words came out. The man was in complete shock. He slowly shook his head. "You are absolutely awful."

Annie couldn't help but laugh. "I know! It was cruel and unusual even for me. The only defense I can claim is that I get very silly when I get tired. Consider yourself forewarned."

"Thanks for the warning," Ryan said sarcastically. "I don't think I want to hear any more of this!" He tried to look serious, but soon they both broke into laughter.

"You know you do," Annie waved a playful finger at him. "You know that I know that you do, so I'm going to continue." Annie laughed again. "So when he asked me for a date Saturday night…"

"You said you were busy." Ryan couldn't contain his laughter anymore.

"That's right. He quickly asked me out for Sunday, and…"

"You said that you were busy!" Ryan was laughing hard now. "I can't believe that you did this. How long did your scam go on for?"

"He asked me out consecutively all the way to the next Thursday! I finally accepted the date on Thursday!" Annie was bubbling over with laughter.

"You are simply terrible! I don't think I want to know you anymore!" Ryan said between fits of laughter. "Did you ever fess up?"

"Oh yeah," Annie waved a hand at him, "right away. I was laughing so hard that Ryan knew that something was up. We went out that Saturday night on our first date."

Ryan Jones sighed loudly. "You mean to tell me that my brother still wanted to date you after you had just put him through the ringer?"

"Apparently so," Annie was still laughing. "We were seldom apart after that, except for me finishing up college. We felt as though we had walked into a fairy tale. We just clicked right away and got along remarkably well. We fell in love very quickly. After about two weeks of dating, we both knew that we were going to get married. And," Annie waved a stern finger at her brother-in-law, "that is why I believe that God didn't allow us to come together earlier. If we had started dating when I was sixteen and he was eighteen, there would have been too many physical temptations. I mean, the man was the love of my life. I was totally smitten, head over heels in love with him from the start. God brought us together in his perfect timing and we married two years later."

"Did you finish college?"

"Yes," Annie nodded her head. "I finished in three years by overloading my courses. I had a very good incentive. My parents didn't want us to get married until I had finished college. We wanted desperately to get married, so I crammed my way through school. We got married the day after I graduated."

"God's timing really is perfect."

"Yes," Annie agreed. "He knows what is best. That's for sure." Annie paused for a moment as a big yawn escaped from her mouth. In a slow sleepy voice she said, "So now you know how we met, you can go to sleep."

"Yeah," Ryan glanced at the clock on the wall, "it's four in the morning and I guess we should try to get some sleep now. Why don't we pray first?"

"Now?" Annie questioned.

"Tomorrow we'll probably be too tired."

Annie nodded and curiously watched as Ryan tenderly took her hand and closed his eyes to pray. In a sincere and grateful way he thanked the Lord for all that had happened in the last few days. He thanked the Lord for Annie and their kids. He prayed for the Lord's peace and guidance during surgery, and then said Amen.

Annie felt too choked up to say much. Ryan Jones had definitely touched her heart these past few days and she felt tearful with emotion. She managed to say a short prayer, and when she closed, Ryan squeezed her hand and they both fell asleep.

Eight

At six o'clock the next morning, the five kids and Gil walked into Ryan's hospital room to find Ryan and Annie fast asleep. "I'm going to head down to the café to get some strong coffee." Gil's voice was groggy and his eyes very heavy. "I think I need to be hot wired this morning to wake up. I'll be back in a few minutes."

Beth looked over at Amy curiously and asked if she thought they should wake them up. Amy nodded. "I think so. The nurse is going to be in soon to prep your dad for surgery. If you want to spend a few minutes with him before his operation, I think you should wake him up now." Beth went over and shook her dad's shoulder lightly. Ryan moaned quietly and then rolled over without ever opening his eyes.

Before Amy could reach her mom, David frantically waved his arms at her. "I know a way that we can wake them up." He had a mischievous smile on his face that an adult never would have trusted. "Channel 62 plays Taps every fifteen

minutes between five and six o'clock. Let's set the
volume up high and walk out."

The kids tuned in Taps, set the volume on the
TV all the way up and walked out of the room. As
the loud bugle music bounced off the walls of the
hospital room, Annie flew out of her recliner chair
and Ryan bolted upright in bed. Their eyes focused
momentarily on the TV, and then to the doorway
where the five kids stood smiling proudly.

A second later, a nurse came flying into the
room, and hit the off switch on the TV. "That was
completely uncalled for." She glared at the kids
menacingly. "You're old enough to know better.
Your father's having heart surgery today. A scare
like that could...I should throw you all out right
now." She turned and studied Ryan intently. "Are
you OK?"

Ryan smiled. "Yeah, I'm OK. It kind of brought
back memories from being at camp."

"Dad," David was in tears, "I'm sorry. It was my
stupid idea. I just wasn't thinking."

"It's OK, David. I'm still ticking." Ryan
thumped his chest lightly. "Besides," he glanced
over at Annie, "I'm sure Annie can help me think of
some creative ways to get you back. She's very
gifted at that sort of thing!" Ryan winked at Annie
and then laughed when he noticed his kids surprised
expressions.

"Amy," Annie ran a hand through her messy hair, "did you bring that change of clothes and that bag of stuff I asked for?"

"Yeah, Mom." Amy picked up a bag and handed it to her.

"Well then, I'm off to freshen up." Annie took her bag and headed for the restroom.

When Annie came back ten minutes later, she found the kids and Gil gathered around Ryan's bed in a prayer circle. She joined the circle and prayed sincerely for her new friend. After they closed in prayer, Amy looked over at her mom. "Mom," she was impressively amazed, "you look great! How do you fix yourself up so nicely in such a short time?"

Annie smiled at her daughter. "Over the years I've learned a few secrets."

"You look wiped." Ryan eyed her with concern.

"Yeah?" Annie looked amused. "Well, someone kept me up until four in the morning talking and talking."

"Dad!" Nicole scolded him, "You were up until four in the morning? You'd bust us if we did that! I should take away your dessert, TV, and telephone privileges. You've been very bad!"

Ryan laughed. His middle daughter was one spunky kid. "You're right. I would bust you if you stayed up until four in the morning-good thing it's me and not you."

"Ha! You're the parent. You should be setting a golden example for me!" Nicole laughed and squeezed her dad's hand. "What were you doing anyways? Pigging out on junk food and watching old movie reruns?"

Ryan smiled at her. "Annie was telling me how she met your Uncle Ryan. You should have her tell the story while I'm in surgery. It's unbelievable!"

Before Annie could comment, an orderly and a nurse came in the room to get Ryan ready for surgery. "Can I have five more minutes with my family?" Ryan flashed the nurse a charming smile and she instantly melted.

"Sure, Ryan, we'll be back in five minutes."

Annie turned so Ryan couldn't see her smile. The man is so full of charm and definitely knows how to use it. He could probably charm the socks off of anyone. He was shameless.

"OK guys," Ryan's voice had become quiet and serious, "I need hugs now. Gather round." Beth, David and Nicole went first, giving their dad big loving hugs. Then Gil stepped forward and gave Ryan a big bear hug and slapped him on the back a few times the way that guys do to each other. Annie and Amy looked at Ryan awkwardly not knowing what to do.

"Come on you two," Ryan's tone was warm and inviting, "when you go for surgery, a hug is required by all family members present. Now step up."

Amy walked over first and gave Ryan a big hug. Annie inched her way nervously over toward Ryan. She felt so much closer to him, but still, they had only known each other for three days. Intimacy always made her feel uncomfortable.

"Annie," Ryan smiled up at her with a teasing expression on his face, "I don't bite. Remember?"

That broke the ice for her. Annie went forward and gave Ryan a big loving hug. She couldn't deny the fact that it felt great to be in his big, loving arms. As she went to pull away, Ryan tightened his grip around her. Annie didn't mind. After a moment, he loosened his arms around her back, and she lifted her head slightly. They were practically nose-to-nose now, and Annie felt totally lost in Ryan's deep blue eyes. Quickly, before Annie could anticipate Ryan's next move, he leaned up toward her and kissed her firmly on the lips. He held the kiss long enough for her sleepy head to realize that it had actually happened. Ryan let his head drop back onto his pillow but continued to hold Annie close. Staring right up into her big brown eyes, he said quietly but confidently, "I love you, Annie."

"OK Ryan," the orderly announced loudly as he walked into the room, "time to rock and roll." He got behind the head of Ryan's bed and rolled him out of the intensely quiet room.

Annie glanced over at the kids and their smiling, glowing faces confirmed to her what had just happened was real. Panic flooded over her like a tidal wave. She felt her world spinning out of control and began to hear a high-pitched noise in her ears. The world around her was going black. Annie made a last ditched effort to grab a chair near her, but it was too late. She passed out cold and was already on her way to the floor.

The next thing Annie was aware of was that someone was shaking her. As she opened her eyes, she saw a very worried Amy hovering over her. "Mom!" Amy's voice was small and frightened. "Are you OK?"

As Annie began to stir, her hand went automatically to her forehead. She felt a sharp pain in her head. The dizziness was returning in waves and it left her feeling weak and nauseous.

"Stay down, Annie," Nurse Carol's tone was commanding. "Don't even try to get up just yet."

"OK," Annie mumbled. As her hand went to her forehead again, she let out a low, painful moan.

"You're going to need stitches Annie." Nurse Carol spoke authoritatively. "The gash on your forehead is deep."

Annie felt Nurse Carol swabbing her forehead and putting on a bandage. "How did this happen?" Nurse Carol asked the kids in an accusing tone. The loud morning bugle solo was still on her mind.

David's face was covered with a wide obnoxious smirk. Amy saw it, and felt the need to protect her mother from embarrassing rumors. "She didn't sleep much last night and she got up too quickly. It made her dizzy and she passed out."

The nurse accepted her statement and nodded her head understandingly. "Annie," Nurse Carol studied her face closely, "do you feel ready to try to sit up?" Annie nodded, and Nurse Carol and Beth helped her up and guided her over to the recliner chair.

"You've got to drink this, Annie." Nurse Carol shoved a cold drink into her hands.

As Annie took a small sip through a bent straw, she gasped and instantly made a miserable puckered face. "Carol," Annie scrunched her face up, "what is this stuff? It tastes awful! Are you trying to kill me?"

Nurse Carol laughed. "No, I'm not trying to kill you, Annie. Our purpose here at Mass General is to help and heal."

Annie laughed. "Then I suggest that you stop serving this sludge. It's terrible!"

"It's a healthy, unsweetened combination of pineapple, grapefruit juice and lime." Nurse Carol was still smiling from the disgusted expression that remained on Annie's face.

"Shoot," Annie grumbled in an exasperated tone, "who cares if this stuff is healthy. It's completely undrinkable. Can't you get me some sweet, sugary junk food drink like Coke or Pepsi?"

"It was the only thing left in the frig," Nurse Carol replied in a matter of fact tone.

Annie laughed. "No wonder! No one is going to volunteer to drink that poison!" Everyone laughed again.

"Annie," Beth touched her shoulder, "I'll run down to the café for you and get something edible."

Annie smiled gratefully at Beth, yet her smile quickly faded as she looked down on her shirt and noticed the blood.

Amy had noticed it too. "Mom, do you want me to go back home and get you some clean clothes?"

"Would you, Honey?" Amy nodded. "That would be great." She squeezed her daughter's hand. "Thanks."

As Amy began to go, Annie grabbed her daughter's hand tightly. "I don't want you driving alone. No one's had much sleep…."

Before Annie could finish her sentence, Gil's deep voice interrupted her. "I'll drive her, Annie." She thanked him and the two of them left.

Wearily, Annie glanced over and eyed Nicole and David. "What just happened with your dad," she was working overtime trying to keep her voice even and not blush like a tomato, "well, it wasn't what it looked like. It wasn't what you thought."

"Oh, yeah," David teased, "I think it was exactly what it looked like and exactly what we thought."

"David," Annie's tone was stern, "your dad was extremely tired and slightly sedated. I don't think he knew what he was doing."

David and Nicole laughed. "I think dad knew exactly what he was doing," Nicole's voice was kind but confident. "It's quite obvious to us that he's taken with you."

Annie looked at her completely horrified. This was definitely not what she wanted to hear.

Nicole went over to Annie and gently touched her arm. "Don't be afraid of him. He's a very godly man. My dad is the most decent man I know."

Just then, Beth came sailing into the room with a large orange juice and a corn muffin. "Here, Annie," she said kindly, "eat this. I think it should taste better than the poison they were trying to give you before."

"Thank you Beth. That was very thoughtful of you."

"Well," Beth smiled widely, "it's the least I can do after what my dad did to you!" The three kids broke up laughing, but Beth stopped after she noticed how Annie paled and stiffened.

"Annie," Beth's tone held alarm, "you're getting pale again. She took the juice from Annie's hands so it wouldn't spill and set it on the table. "Listen," Beth stated firmly to her younger brother and sister, "drop the subject now. It's upsetting Annie." They quickly apologized and Annie smiled at them weakly.

Nurse Carol marched back into the room and looked at Annie, and then over to the food that Beth had gotten for her. "It looks good, Annie, but it would look even better to me if you were actually eating it!"

Nurse Carol took the juice off the table and handed it to Annie. "Try a little, will you?" Annie nodded and took a sip. "We need to get some food in you and then wheel you down to the ER. We have a doctor waiting there to stitch you up."

"Oh, Carol," Annie asked dreadfully, "is it really necessary?"

"Yes," Carol answered determinedly. "House rule number one here is, If it bleeds, we have to stop it and clean it up. And," Nurse Carol stated as she wiggled her eyebrow back and forth like Groucho Marks, "if you're a good girl, you might even get a lollipop."

"Come on, Carol," Annie's tone was annoyed, "I've had worse cuts than this on the playground. This is no big deal."

"Annie," Carol replied with clear cut authority in her voice, "this is my playground, and you're going to get stitched up whether you like it or not. The bandage isn't even stopping the bleeding."

"You should try duct tape," Annie said seriously. "That stuff is amazing."

Nurse Carol stared at her hard for a moment. "If you give me any more grief, I may try the duct tape across your mouth."

Annie's mouth swung open in shock. "That definitely would not be nice of you."

"Annie," Carol was losing her patience, "they don't pay me here to be nice. They pay me to take care of you and that's what I'm going to do. Got it?"

"Yes, Ma'am," Annie said quickly. It's hard to argue with a drill Sergeant especially if she is the one running the battleground. Annie knew when it was time to toss the towel in.

A few minutes later, another nurse came through the door pushing a wheelchair. "Your chariot awaits, My Lady," she said pleasantly.

"Oh," Annie immediately waved off the chair ride, "I really don't need to ride in that." Annie saw Carol's eyes narrow, and immediately changed her mind. "But I could, I mean, if you think it's a good idea."

"That's a good girl," Carol patted Annie on the shoulder. "Just maybe you'll get that lollipop after all."

Beth volunteered to drive Annie down to the ER. As she grabbed the handles on the wheelchair, she glared at her brother and sister and said pointedly, "You two STAY!"

David let out a loud woof sound.

"You're so immature," Beth complained.

"Hey! I'm a sixteen year old guy," David's voice was full of humor, "I'm suppose to be immature!" Annie, Beth and Nicole just laughed. Maybe he was immature but he was a good source of comic relief.

As Beth pushed Annie toward the ER, she chatted away cheerfully. She told Annie all about their ranch in Chatfield Hollow. "You'd love it there. Tennessee is a beautiful state but I have always thought that Chatfield Hollow was it's special jewel. The area is so gorgeous with its mountains, meadows, rivers and lakes. You'll have to come for a visit sometime."

Annie nodded slightly and quietly agreed that she'd like that. Too many issues were parading through her mind at the moment to put much thought into any one of them. She felt like the last few days had flooded her emotionally and physically.

After Beth rolled Annie into the empty elevator, she came around and knelt down in front of her. "Annie," her voice was urgent, "I'm sorry this happened to you. I really am."

Annie squeezed Beth's hands lovingly and the young woman's eyes began to overflow with tears.

"I want you to understand something," Beth was looking directly into Annie's eyes. "Dad is not a ladies' man. He's not the type of guy to come on to a woman. Boy," Beth pushed some loose strands of hair out of her face, "if he was, he wouldn't have to try very hard. You wouldn't believe how some women throw themselves at him. It's horrible! And," Beth's eyes narrowed, "they know better. They're supposed to be Christians!"

Annie nodded understandingly. "Christians are supposed to walk a different path than the world, but sometimes they don't. There are so many ways to be tempted off the right path that I think, as Christians, we need to try even harder to guard ourselves."

"Annie," Beth said lovingly, "I really believe that dad meant exactly what he said to you. I haven't seen him this lit up since mom. You," Beth laid a hand on Annie's arm, "are the first woman he's shown interest in since my mom."

Annie just looked at Beth. "I honestly don't know what to say."

"You don't need to say anything," Beth smiled kindly at her. "I just wanted you to know that it's OK with me; you know," she shrugged her shoulders, "whatever happens between you and my dad."

"Now I really don't know what to say." Annie shut her eyes for a moment feeling overwhelmed.

After a doctor had given Annie twelve stitches in her forehead, and medication to ease her pounding headache, Annie was returned to the comfort of her recliner and fell fast asleep.

By the time she awoke, several hours later, Ryan was back in the room. She glanced over at him, full of relief that he was back. She couldn't help but study his rhythmic breathing for a while. After a few minutes she concluded that things seemed normal, and soon her own weariness returned, and she drifted off to sleep again.

Annie slept straight through the night and did not wake up until early the next morning. As she looked over at Ryan, she saw he was still sleeping. She quietly picked up a bag of clean clothes that Amy had brought her, and headed off for the shower down the hall.

By the time she got back to the room, Ryan, his kids, Gil, and Amy were gathered around his bed. They were talking quietly, but whatever the topic of conversation was, must have been humorous because their faces were lit with amusement. When Ryan saw Annie, he immediately waved her over to his bedside. He patted the side of his bed gently indicating for her to sit down. He appeared as though he were trying very hard to suppress his laughter. Annie could make out the beginnings of a grin that was tugging on the corners of his mouth. It looked like it was dying to pop out. As she noticed his blue eyes dancing with amusement, her own eyes instinctively narrowed. "What?" she asked him cautiously.

"So, what did you do yesterday?"

He was trying to act too casual, and the pieces quickly fell together for her. Now she understood the grins and she quickly cast a cold hard stare at the kids and Gil. They broke up laughing and Annie moved off the bed to the security of her own chair.

"Please, Annie," Ryan patted his bed, "come back and sit over here."

As soon as she sat down on the side of the bed, Ryan's hand went slowly up to her forehead. He gently pushed her brown bangs aside and studied the bandage covering her stitches. His intense eyes went from her forehead to her eyes. He held them for a moment with his own. In a choked up voice he told her how sorry he was.

"It's not your fault, Ryan. I was just very tired."

Ryan nodded and then took Annie's hand and gave it a tender squeeze. He smiled at her even though the tears were still clouding his eyes. "That's not the usual response I get when I tell a woman that I love her." His voice had an element of teasing in it, but overall it was far too serious for Annie.

The whole room broke out with laughter except for Annie. She barely heard them. Her mind was so focused on Ryan's face. She always felt that you could tell what was going on in a person's heart by looking at the expression in their eyes. Right now, Ryan was looking at her with so much love and tenderness that she felt numb and completely off balance.

"We were both very tired last night." Annie said trying to dismiss the incident. "Let's just forget about it."

Ryan didn't answer but continued to look at Annie. She would have gotten to her feet and run away if she could have felt them. Everything about her felt numb. The only thing that she could feel was the erratic pounding of her own heart.

Annie finally managed to pop out of her own trance long enough to look away. She had to look away from Ryan. His gaze was so tender and loving that it was almost melting her. His eyes were filled to overflowing with a love for her that she didn't want to admit existed. She knew she was in big trouble. Whether or not she wanted his love, or wanted to admit or deny it's existence, seemed irrelevant at this point. His love was there, shining out for the entire world to see. There was no way she could deny it any longer, and a new sense of panic washed over her as she knew that she didn't have a clue as to what she was going to do about it.

Nine

Ryan, David and Gil spent the next two weeks at Annie's Stony Brook Farm.

Ryan enjoyed spending time at Annie's farm. It was autumn in New England and the leaves were at their peak in Boston. During those late September days, the red, orange and yellow leaves were practically glowing with color. Everywhere you looked, the landscape had exploded into a fiery, awesome, brilliant bouquet of colors. Ryan felt as though he were observing the masterpiece of a talented, gifted artist. No one could ever compete with God's artwork. The beauty took his breath away, and he had no trouble understanding why fall was Annie's favorite time of the year.

Ryan went for daily checkups at Dr. Thatcher's office and grew steadily stronger every day. The recovery process consisted of a routine set of exercises. The physical therapy was going well for Ryan and he thanked the Lord every day that he had been given more time on earth. He had been granted a second chance at life and it was a gift that he took quite seriously. It was extremely difficult for his kids to go through life without their mom. They had come close to losing their father as well. He closed his eyes for a moment. He couldn't even imagine the depth of pain they would have gone through if he had died. It was not the time for him or for his kids to have to go through that type of pain. Losing one parent was hard enough to deal with; losing two seemed cruel and impossibly difficult. He thanked God again that it was not a situation that his kids would have to face right now. Life was a gift and time was something that should be valued and treasured.

He knew the last week had changed his perspective on life. He had been given a crash course on just how fragile life was. It was as though someone had taken the blinders off him and he could clearly see. Things had changed for him and he knew he would never look at life quite the same. He didn't want to go through life just existing from one day to the next. He didn't want to hide in the safety and comfort of routine. He wanted his life to matter. He wanted to step outside his personal comfort zone and let God work in his heart with no strings attached. He wanted his life to count for God. He knew that if he was living his life sold out for God, it would mean that he was giving God, and all those around him, the very best of himself that he could give. That would be living. That would be life.

Annie often accompanied Ryan on his daily walk and was always encouraged as she watched his progress. It didn't take long for her to learn that her brother in law was an incredibly determined person. He pushed himself through his exercises, day after day, even when he looked like he was ready to collapse.

One day, after his exercise routine, Ryan was a little more tired than usual. He went into the den to rest on the couch and Annie took the opportunity to get some baking done. She wanted to take Ryan on a picnic later and thought some of her famous Reese's peanut butter cookies would be great to bring along. As she started grabbing ingredients from her kitchen cabinets, her mind started thinking about Ryan Jones, which, actually wasn't too unusual because she found that was what her mind wanted to think about most these days. He filled her every thought, and she found it both pleasing and annoying. As Annie started chopping up Reese peanut butter cups, the sound of laughter from the doorway made her turn.

"You're the first person that I've met that holds a steady conversation with herself." Ryan had a huge smirk across his face and looked quite pleased with his discovery.

"Are you saying that I talk to myself?" Annie tried to sound bold, but it was hard to when she could feel the embarrassment flood her face to a toasty shade of beet red. She knew that she did talk to herself. She had ever since childhood, but to be caught doing so in front of Ryan was humiliating.

Ryan laughed at her again. "Annie, not only do you talk to yourself, but you have full running dialogues going on. It's pretty interesting to try to follow."

Annie sighed loudly. "Listen, I may occasionally think out loud…."

"You," he pointed an accusing finger directly at her, "were talking to yourself. I know what I heard. It's too late to try to deny it."

The humor written all over his face was starting to annoy Annie. She tried to stare Ryan down but it only made him laugh harder.

"Now Annie," he took a step closer to her, "do you honestly think that little glare of yours is going to frighten me?"

Annie had to laugh. The man was impossible, and wonderful, and she didn't have a clue as to what she was going to do about it. "I sometimes talk out loud when I'm thinking or praying." Annie paused and grabbed another Reese out of the package to chop up for her cookies. "Besides," she turned and looked at him again, "you wouldn't have heard anything if you hadn't been sneaking up on me like that."

Ryan laughed loudly. "I wasn't sneaking up on you Annie." His grin was growing wider as he talked. "I was walking into your kitchen like I always do, and, you would have heard me if you hadn't been talking to yourself so loudly. You were totally absorbed there. Besides," he winked playfully at her, "I would have said something, but I thought it would have been rude of me to interrupt."

Annie narrowed her eyes at him. "Go away!"

"I can't," Ryan walked toward her. "I have no place to go."

"Then I'll go," Annie put her Reese down.

"You can't." Ryan scanned the ingredients on the counter. "You've got to finish whatever it is you're baking. It looks good."

"Do you promise not to bug me?" Annie threw her hands on her hips trying to act tough.

Ryan smiled charmingly at her. "Now, I'm not about to go ahead and make a promise that I know I won't be able to keep."

"That's what I thought. You stay, I'll go." Annie felt irritated. It wasn't Ryan that bothered her; it was more her reaction to him. He simply set her off. He seemed to know how to affect her deep down, and right at the moment she didn't want to be affected deep down or otherwise.

"Cool your heals, Annie," Ryan said easily. "You keep making whatever it is you're making, and I'll fix us both some coffee."

As Annie went about collecting the rest of the ingredients out of the pantry, she noticed Ryan opening and closing the cabinets, getting out the coffee and the filters. It suddenly struck her that they were beginning to know each other's domestic habits. They worked in the kitchen together, like clockwork, complementing each other as if they had been doing it all their lives. Ryan even got out the cocoa and the caramels that she liked to add to her coffee. They were coming to learn what each other liked, and the panic rising inside of Annie was numbing. It all seemed too intimate. The idea of intimacy was fine as long as it was just an idea. Once the idea became a reality, it scared her to death.

Ryan chose that moment to casually turn and glance at Annie. She quickly erased the frightened expression off her face, but not before Ryan caught it. Annie narrowed her eyes defensively at him. He knew that Annie was the type of person that would think and rethink every aspect of every situation she allowed herself to go into. He knew, without a doubt, that this time the situation was him, and he was being examined in a very thorough, meticulous process. She was not a spontaneous person and never allowed herself to go into new situations blindly. He silently prayed that her fear would not build such a wall between them that it couldn't be taken down.

Ryan smiled at her tenderly trying to ease her heart and mind. Annie's eyes clouded over with tears, and she quickly turned away. "I'll be back in a minute."

As Annie exited the room, Amy came flying in. She surveyed the mess on the counter and then smiled. "Oh, you're in for a treat. Mom's making her Reese cookies. They're so good."

"I think your mom's addicted to chocolate and peanut butter." Ryan laughed quietly as he looked at the chopped up Reese on the counter.

"Yeah," Amy smiled back at him "if you want to bring her something special, skip the flowers and bring her anything with chocolate and peanut butter in it. She'll love you!"

Ryan smiled and nodded. "Thanks for the tip. By the way," he picked up a Reese and tossed it over to Amy, "I've got something that I've been wanting to ask you."

"Shoot." Amy quickly unwrapped her Reese cup.

"Why doesn't your mom date at all? I remember the speech that she gave me when I first met her about never dating again because she wasn't planning on getting remarried, but," Ryan paused for a minute and played absent-minded with a

Reese's wrapper, "I just feel like there's got to be more to the story than what she's saying."

"I think you should be asking me that question." Annie was standing in the doorway with her hands planted defensively on her hips. It didn't take a PhD in Psychology to figure out that she was clearly annoyed with him.

Ryan studied her for a moment, and then said thoughtfully, "OK. Why don't you date?"

Annie blew out a loud frustrated breath. "That's none of your business."

Ryan smiled at her. "That's what I thought you'd say, and, that's why I was asking your daughter."

Annie's eyes were shooting electric sparks at him. "You think you can dig through my personal life like it's some kind of cheap magazine. Out of the blue, you waltz into my life. You think that you can knock down the wall around my heart that I have so carefully built. It's there for my protection, Ryan, and it's not coming down."

Ryan stared at her a full second before replying. "Call me Joshua, and, think of yourself as Jericho. The wall is coming down Annie, whether you like it or not. I'm just the Joshua in your life. God is the one who wants to knock your wall down. Don't kill the messenger."

"I don't like it one bit!"

"I just want to get to know you better. That's not an easy thing." He sighed loudly and looked at Annie seriously. "If you don't want to discuss something, you can always tell me to take a hike."

"I've been telling you to take a hike for weeks, and look at all the good it's done." Annie smiled at the irony of it.

Ryan grinned at her proudly. "I don't scare off that easily."

Annie had to laugh. "That's true." She didn't know what to do with him. She never did. She figured that the best evasive tactic would be to get back to her cookies. If she kept herself busy, she wouldn't have to think about Ryan so much. Then she remembered lunch and silently groaned. She just couldn't get away from him. In a voice as normal and calm as possible, Annie asked Ryan what he wanted for lunch.

"I'm not fussy," he shrugged his broad shoulders. "Whatever you're having is fine with me."

Annie laughed. "What do you think about peanut butter and jelly?"

Ryan's eyebrows shot up. "For who?" He scrunched his face up. "A little kid that is going to preschool with a lunch box that has a superhero on the side of it?"

Annie and Amy both laughed hard. "Good one, Uncle Ryan." Amy scooped up a handful of Reese. "Sorry to eat and run, but David, Gil and I are watching an intense football game."

"Who's playing?" Ryan asked in a curious tone.

"The New England Patriots and the Tennessee Titans." Amy didn't even try to hide the big smile that was plastered across her face.

Ryan smiled back, taking up the challenge that he saw in her eyes. Both of their local teams were playing each other and there was no doubt in either of their minds which side of the fence they were on, or who they were cheering for. The battle lines were clearly drawn, and they stood opposite each other, proudly defending their own team.

"Who's winning?" Ryan's eyes narrowed at Amy.

Amy laughed loudly. "Look at this big, happy smile on my face and that should tell you who's winning," Amy's voice was bold and sassy. "Oh," she suddenly grabbed a box of tissues off the counter, "I'd better bring these. David's going to need these to dry his tears when the Patriots crush the Titans into the ground for good."

Amy and Annie howled with laughter as Ryan just stood there drumming his fingers on the kitchen counter. As Amy disappeared into the den, Ryan directed his attention to Annie. "She is one feisty girl. She's not very sympathetic to the agony of defeat."

Annie laughed. "And the reason that surprises you is…." She waved her hand in the air as if she were searching for the right answer.

They both laughed. "Like mother, like daughter," Ryan teased.

"Well, the apples usually don't fall too far from the tree."

"She has a lot of you in her."

"So I've been told," Annie smiled warmly.

"What were we talking about before Amy rubbed my nose in the dirt about my team losing to her team?"

"Peanut butter and jelly sandwiches," Annie smirked at him.

"For who?" Ryan asked looking at her closely.

Annie smiled at him. "For you. I'll even run down into the basement and see if I can find a lunch box with a superhero on it. I want you to have the full experience."

Ryan laughed. "I haven't eaten peanut butter and jelly since I was a kid, but, I bet I would look pretty cute carrying the lunch box around."

"I bet you'd look cute carrying the lunch box around too. After all those years of neglect, I bet you're just craving a good peanut butter and jelly sandwich!"

Ryan laughed. "Can't you make anything else?"

"Sure," Annie scooped up some cookie dough and put it on the cookie sheets, "I make a mean peanut butter and M&M sandwich. It's really great for the person on the go, because in one sandwich you get both your meal and dessert!"

"You're kidding?" Ryan sounded repulsed.

"They're really good," Annie popped the cookie tray into the oven. "I've been making peanut butter and M&M sandwiches for years."

"Don't you have anything to feed big boys? I'm a man," Ryan brought his arms above his shoulders and flexed them. "I need some meat in my sandwich."

Annie gazed thoughtfully at him. "Well," she poked her head in the refrigerator, "I've got ham and turkey in here, but it's not nearly as good as peanut butter and M&M." She looked at Ryan seriously. "That's what I'd recommend, but it is your choice."

Ryan's mouth dropped open. "You mean to tell me," he said slowly advancing toward her, "that you had ham and turkey in there all the time, and you were going to fed me some sloppy, goopy little kid's sandwich?"

Annie ditched her attacker by stepping around to the other side of the counter. "That was basically the plan. I figured that if I fed you too good, you might never leave."

Ryan's smile quickly faded from his face. "I may never leave anyway," he whispered just loud enough for her to hear. "I'm having too much fun here."

Now it was Annie's mouth that dropped open in shock. The man never ceased to surprise her. In a calculated move, she turned away from him and back to her cookies. As she mechanically started dropping dough on the sheet, she tried to regain her composure. Ryan had a way of taking her off guard and leaving her that way. The bell went off, and she grabbed the potholders and took the first batch of cookies out of the oven and put the second one in.

"I was going to make sandwiches," Annie willed her voice to sound normal, "and take you on a picnic. You've been working so hard that I figured you could use a change of scenery."

"That sounds great! I'll make the sandwiches for our date." Ryan took the bread out of the breadbox. "You finish up the cookies. They smell delicious."

Annie spun around to face him. "I don't mind making the sandwiches, but for your information, this is not a date."

"I'd rather make them myself, Annie," Ryan laughed. "I don't want you sticking peanut butter or M&M's in them. And," he tossed her a dazzling smile, "why isn't this a date? Two adults going on a picnic sounds like a date to me."

Annie sighed. "I'm not dating anyone," she stated emphatically. "I thought I made that clear to you."

Ryan stopped what he was doing and turned and looked directly at her. "I want to date you," he said gently but persistently.

Annie was starting to feel her temper rise. "I want to drive a Porsche but hey, we don't all get what we want. That's life."

Ryan studied Annie thoughtfully. If he pushed her too hard he was going to lose her. He had to remind himself that even Joshua had to march around Jericho for a week before God knocked the wall down. He knew that knocking Annie's wall down would take a lot longer than Jericho, but he also knew that God would give him patience. In the meantime, the chemistry between them was so hot it sizzled. Every time they were together, sparks flew. There was a bond that couldn't be denied, but at this point couldn't be pursued either. Once again, Ryan got the feeling that the only thing he could do concerning him and Annie was pray. God was going to have to help her deal with her fears. He would be there to help, but God was the only one who could heal Annie's heart.

When they finished making their picnic lunch, Annie went into the den and asked David, Gil, and

Amy if they'd like to go. They all declined. The Titans were making a comeback against the Patriots and none of them wanted to miss the game. Annie understood. She told them to help themselves to the sandwiches in the frig when they were ready.

She led Ryan out to the barn, and when she opened the door, a loud gasp escaped from his mouth. There in front of them, was Ryan Smith's 1965 Ford Shelby Mustang. It was washed and polished and looked ready to roll.

Ryan slowly made his way toward the black sports car with the wide white racing stripes. "It looks in mint condition." Ryan excitedly examined the car.

"It's in pretty good shape," Annie laughed, "though it may not be when I get done driving it."

"Ryan looked at her with an amused smirk dancing across his face. "We're going in the Mustang?"

"Yep," Annie winked at him. "I thought I'd take you to Boston's North Shore for a picnic."

"The beach?" Ryan sounded thrilled, like a little kid waiting to build a sand castle.

"Yes," Annie smiled at him. "It's a mandatory policy that all guests here at Stony Brook go to the ocean."

"Good policy."

"Make yourself comfortable in the passenger seat while I load the picnic supplies in the trunk."

Ryan glanced at the passenger seat and then back at Annie. He had just assumed that she'd let him drive. The ride into Boston was still giving him nightmares. "You're driving?" Ryan couldn't hide the concern in his tone.

"Of course, silly. It's too long to walk." Ryan's face radiated concern. "Listen, if you'd rather not go we can stay and watch the rest of the game with the kids."

"I want to go," Ryan answered honestly, "I just don't want you driving me."

Annie's eyes narrowed. The anticipation of war hung in the air.

"The ride to Boston in rush hour traffic with you is an experience that I don't want to repeat in my lifetime."

Annie glared at him. "It's slow back roads all the way. Do you think you can handle that?" She didn't like being hassled about her driving.

"Annie," Ryan laughed, "there is nothing slow about this car or you!"

Annie had to smile. He was right. "I'll do my best to keep it under the speed of light. Does that sound fair?"

Ryan laughed again and settled into the black bucket seat. "What sounds fair to me Annie, is that if you scare me with your driving, I'm going to steal the keys from you and lock you in the trunk."

Annie's mouth swung open. "Man, you really aren't used to driving in the city. Are you?"

"Annie," Ryan strapped his seatbelt in place and prayed that it worked well, "I believe we've had this conversation before." He turned and looked at her and she just looked right back. "I have traveled around the world, and driven in many cities. Nothing has scared me more than the way you drove through Boston. You're a nut."

Annie decided it was best to drop the conversation. It was going nowhere fast. She turned the key, and the big engine roared to life.

"I love that sound!" Ryan smiled as he laid his head back against the seat.

"Me too!" Annie put the car into first gear and they took off. As they made their way down the narrow, winding, back roads of New England, Ryan felt like he had been put on an amusement park ride. Annie drove the Mustang skillfully, hugging the curving roads tightly as if the car were on rails. She shifted smoothly through the gears and commanded the car with ease. Yet, Ryan thought, as he instinctively gripped the sides of his seat, she drove fast, like she was on a racetrack, competing with the other drivers on the road for the lead spot. He was already making plans in his mind to steal the keys from her. He was driving home, even if that included knocking Annie out. It was worth the risk because he had a strong desire to arrive back at Stony Brook alive. He knew he was being picky, he thought sarcastically, but with Annie's driving, it was only a matter of time before he would end up six feet under or have a heart attack. It was an awful experience to endure.

As Annie whizzed onto North Shore road, she looked over at Ryan excitedly. "This road will take us right along the ocean until we reach the beach. I think you'll find it interesting."

Ryan nodded. "What's Tyler like? You haven't mentioned much about him."

"I can't remember what I've already told you about him," Annie answered thoughtfully. "The last few weeks have been pretty crazy." Ryan nodded. "Tyler is twenty. He's in the Coast Guard, stationed in New London, Connecticut. His ship is out to sea, that's why you haven't met him yet. He's a great guy," Annie smiled. "I'm so proud of him. There's a picture in my wallet of Tyler. Why don't you dig it out?"

Ryan fumbled through her wallet and found a snapshot that looked like a high school graduation picture. "He looks very tall," Ryan's voice was a bit weary. "A lot taller than me!"

Annie laughed. "He is tall. Ty is 6'9" but don't worry," Annie teased, "we've taught him to play nice with others."

"Very funny," Ryan laughed. As he studied the picture further, he smiled at Tyler's strong family resemblance. "He really looks quite a bit like your husband."

"And you and David," Annie added quickly. "He inherited that beautiful dark hair and those deep blue eyes."

"Yeah, but he's a lot taller than I am. How tall was my brother?"

"Oh," Annie paused for thoughtfully, "probably a few inches taller than you. He was about 6'4"."

"Taller, huh?" The enthusiasm had drained completely out of Ryan's voice.

"Yeah, I guess you were the runt of the litter!"

"Runt! I would hardly call 6'2" a runt!"

Annie laughed at the indignation in his voice. "You know I'm just teasing you."

"You do that a lot." He turned in his seat and smiled at her. "Don't you?"

"I'm afraid so," she laughed quietly, "but I think I'm going to have to be more careful around you."

Ryan raised his eyebrows questioningly at her. "And why is that?"

"You're more outgoing and mischievous than your brother was. I have the feeling that you'd be more likely to throw the jokes back my way a lot quicker."

Ryan laughed. "That's true," he wiggled his eyebrows at her, "so, you'd better watch out!"

They laughed again, and then Annie eased the Mustang to the side of the road. "This is a good place to stop for a bit and watch the boats on the ocean. The traffic's pretty heavy out there today."

Ryan noticed the oil tankers, fishing boats and a bunch of smaller sailboats. He felt like he could hang out here for hours and watch the boats. "When does Tyler's ship come back to port?"

"He's scheduled back the end of October," Annie replied a little distantly. It was always hard for her when Ty was away.

"I'm looking forward to meeting him sometime, but I guess it won't be this visit." Disappointment hung in Ryan's voice and it touched Annie's heart that he cared.

"Another time," Annie said seriously. Ryan, David, and Gil were scheduled to leave at the end of the week. He had to get back to his Tennessee ranch, and more importantly, his music. "We're going to miss you," Annie whispered.

Ryan smiled so tenderly at her that it almost made her heart stop. "Me too. But," he touched her hand lightly for a moment, "the kids and I are already making plans for you, Amy and Tyler to join us in Chatfield Hollow for Christmas."

"Really?"

"Yep," Ryan said playfully, "and you can't say no."

"I'm not sure that we can say yes," Annie answered reluctantly. "We've made tentative plans to spend Christmas with my brother and his family in Maine. I would feel kind of funny backing out on them."

"You have already made plans for Christmas? It's only the end of September."

Annie nodded thoughtfully. "I know," she smiled at him gently. "We tend to make our plans early."

"I'll say." Ryan was quiet for only a moment before he burst out excitedly, "Hey! They can come too! The ranch house is plenty big enough to hold an army. This will be great!"

"I don't know," Annie furrowed her brow in concentration. As her forehead wrinkled, she felt her scar tighten. She instinctively put her hand up to it while she was thinking.

Ryan took her hand down, and then with his other hand gently pushed her bangs aside. He studied the scar carefully and then took his hand away. He sighed heavily and then shook his head slowly.

Annie knew he was blaming himself. "Ryan," she touched his arm, "it's no big deal. I already had a scar on my forehead before," she shrugged her shoulders, "now I have two."

Ryan immediately pushed her bangs back again and looked at the other scar. "How did you get that?"

Annie laughed. "The first time that your brother told me that he loved me, I passed out cold, and cracked my head open like an egg against a rock."

"No way…." Ryan was stunned.

"No," Annie laughed. "I just couldn't resist."

Ryan glared at her though narrow eyes. "You are so not funny, Annie."

"Thank you," Annie smiled back proudly.

He looked at her and laughed. "There's never a dull moment with you around. So, how did you get that scar?"

"I was ten and it was wintertime and my brother and I were sledding." Annie's voice grew reminiscing. "I idolized Bob and wanted to do everything that he did. So when we were sledding through the apple orchard…."

Ryan interrupted her. "You were sledding through an apple orchard? Were you crazy?"

"Not at all," Annie laughed at his expression of disbelief, "I happen to be an extremely good sled driver."

Ryan put his hand back up to Annie's forehead and looked at the scar again. "Good sled driver, huh?" His tone was dripping with skepticism.

"Yes," Annie raised her chin up defiantly, "I was and probably still am. But anyway," Annie looked away from Ryan to ignore his dubious expression, "my brother popped his sled over a snow jump, and I thought I could do the same thing. Yet, instead of going over it," Annie laughed, "I went head on into it."

Ryan's mouth dropped open. "That must have hurt."

"It did," she quickly agreed with him. "You know, it's really not a good idea to try to sled through an ice bank. It doesn't work very well."

"Thanks for the tip." Ryan laughed loudly. "I'll try to remember that for future reference."

Annie started up the Mustang and they drove for about fifteen minutes along the ocean side road. As they rounded a sharp corner, a large concrete lighthouse came into view.

"A lighthouse!" Ryan proclaimed excitedly.

"Very good!" Annie patted his leg condescendingly as if he were a preschool kid. Ryan glared at her but she ignored him. "We're going to eat on the rocks over there by the lighthouse."

"Great!"

As they took the short walk down the sandy beach toward the lighthouse, Ryan eyed the tall structure with awe. "This thing is huge!" He placed a flattened hand against it and let his eyes roam up to the top.

Annie nodded. "Yeah, it's over ninety feet tall."

Annie spread a red and black plaid blanket on the sand between the rocks and the lighthouse. Ryan sat down on it and stretched out leisurely on his side, gazing out to sea. "This is a wonderful spot. Thanks for sharing it with me."

Annie smiled a little shyly under Ryan's intense but loving gaze. "It's always been one of my personal favorites."

They dug into their picnic lunch enthusiastically. They ate ham sandwiches that Ryan had made, along with chips, Annie's special Reese cookies, delicious in season New England apples, and Cokes to drink.

"So," Ryan asked in a laid back voice, as he watched a large sailboat glide by them, "are you going to the Christian Book Awards banquet? Most writers that I know seem to go to that. It seems like it's more of a family reunion among writers than an awards banquet."

Annie smiled as she thought of all her writer friends. They were like family and the banquet was a time that she normally looked forward to. Yet, she thought grimly, as her smile faded from her face, this year was going to be different. Getting all decked out in fancy clothes made her uncomfortable. Heels and long gowns were a far cry from the sneakers, jeans, and tee shirts that she normally wore. And if that wasn't bad enough, she was up for an award and it was making her a nervous wreck. She had tried for over a month to come up with a legitimate excuse for not going, yet she hadn't been able to find one.

She glanced back at Ryan and saw the heated look in his eyes. He was staring at her, and by the intense expression in his eyes, he had been for some time. Annie grumbled under her breath. "Do you have to stare at me like that?"

A long, lazy smile spread slowly across Ryan's face. "No, but I enjoy watching you. You're somewhat of a mystery to me and I find myself very attracted to you."

Annie gave him a cold hard stare. She hated being stared at. "No mystery here. I'm not interested. Got it?"

Ryan's smile grew even wider. "I've got it, but I don't believe you."

"You're infuriating!" Annie mumbled through clenched teeth.

"So I've been told." Ryan smiled at her charmingly.

"So I guess that hearing it again doesn't really affect you much."

"Not much." Ryan laughed loudly. "So, are you going to the banquet?"

"Yes," Annie replied hesitantly. "I decided to go even though I wasn't planning on it." He looked at her curiously, and she continued. "Those award banquets make me so nervous. I'm not really a fancy dress up type of person. I'm more of a jeans and tee shirt type of girl."

Ryan nodded understandingly. "Yeah, I hear you. I'm definitely more comfortable in my jeans and tee shirts than in a suit or tux."

Ryan looked out at the ocean for a moment before turning his attention back to Annie. "Annie," he gave her a dazzling smile, "do you need a date for the banquet?"

"No," Annie answered without further explanation.

"No?" Ryan repeated in a puzzled tone, leaning closer to her. "What do you mean by no?" He appeared half curious and half jealous and Annie couldn't help but laugh at him.

"No," she tried to say as casually as she could, "I'm all set. Thanks." Annie knew that she was starting to drive Ryan crazy and for some reason she really enjoyed it.

"All set." He wrinkled his brow at her.

"Yes, I already have a gentleman accompanying me, but thanks for your concern."

"A gentleman?" His eyes narrowed at her. "And just who is this gentleman?"

"Why should I tell you?" Annie asked with a twinkle in her eye.

"Because," Ryan was exasperated, and spread his arms open wide, "I'm your brother in law. I should protect you from gentleman callers."

Annie laughed so hard she had to set down her can of coke. She was afraid she'd spill it all over herself. Ryan looked at her with a wounded expression on his face. "Ryan, I have the feeling that your way of protecting me from gentleman callers would be to chase them all away!" Annie broke out laughing again and Ryan had to join her.

"So," he asked innocently, "what's wrong with that?"

Annie looked at him and laughed again. Even though his face was calm, she knew, underneath, that he was completely serious about chasing her gentleman callers away. He reminded her of the calm before the storm.

"Besides," he narrowed his eyes again at her, "I thought you were never getting married again."

"I'm not." Annie didn't like where this was going.

"Then why are you dating this gentleman caller?"

"Ryan," Annie was growing impatient with him, "I'm not dating him. He is simply accompanying me to the awards banquet. You're supposed to bring an escort."

Ryan studied her for a minute and then took a large bite out of his apple. He noisily chewed it while studying her thoughtfully.

"We should head back to the farm." Annie started to repack the picnic.

"No! No!" Ryan's façade of calmness instantly evaporated. "Not until you tell me who your date is."

"Ryan," Annie asked pointedly, "why is it so important to you?"

"Because it is." Ryan fiddled with the corner of the blanket. "Do you like this guy?" He was beginning to sound like a nervous schoolboy.

"Absolutely. I wouldn't have asked him if I didn't."

"You asked him?"

Annie nodded.

"Yeah, but you don't love him or anything. Do you?"

"To be honest with you Ryan, I have always loved him, and, I always will." Annie couldn't suppress her laughter anymore.

"Something funny is going on here." Ryan stood up and brushed the crumbs off himself. "What's up?"

"Ryan, I'm going with Tyler to the banquet." Annie smiled kindly at him. "Tyler is the one who is escorting me."

Ryan's mouth dropped open. Annie's laughter could be heard halfway down the beach. "You mean Tyler, as in your son Tyler?" Ryan stared at her in disbelief. Annie nodded and laughed again as she picked up the picnic basket.

"Why, Annie," Ryan smiled slowly, "you are such a tease. You really had me going there! Tyler…" he shook his head and then let out a loud laugh. "You shouldn't make me suffer like that."

Annie laughed. "Aren't artists supposed to suffer? You know, the whole poor and starving artist thing?"

"What you are putting me through," Ryan's voice was far too serious for her, "is cruel and usual treatment, even for an artist."

Ryan looped his arm through Annie's as they strolled back to the Mustang. "You know," he leaned down and whispered into her ear, "that wasn't very nice of you."

"You are entirely too noisy!" She turned and looked at him. "Why does this matter to you so much anyway?"

Ryan paused and took both of Annie's hands in his own. In a tender voice, he spoke quietly but confidently. "If you're honest with yourself, you'll know why it is so important to me. I would tell you, but," his blue eyes twinkled mischievously at her, "I don't want you to pass out again."

Annie went pale and Ryan did two things. He instantly put an arm around her for support and he grabbed the keys out of her hand. When she looked up at him questioningly, he simply laughed. "I am driving home Annie." He opened the passenger door for her. "Would you like to ride with me? I drive a bit slower, but I promise we'll get there eventually."

Ryan laughed loudly and Annie hit him in the shoulder as she got into the car. Ryan went around the car and triumphantly claimed the driver's seat. He smiled at Annie victoriously.

"You're giving me indigestion," Annie nervously played with the ring on her finger.

"Sorry." Ryan was completely insincere.

"You know," Annie began irritated, "my world was running just fine before I met you. I was a happy, content woman."

Ryan pinned her with his eyes. "Then you're contented too easily." A smile broke through his serious expression, and his tone became lighter. "Your expectations are too low. I'm about to raise them."

Annie just stared back at him. The nerve of this man was beyond belief. "You are overconfident, arrogant, and presume far too much when it comes to me."

Ryan glared at her sternly. "Maybe your head believes that, but I don't think that your heart does. I'm confident, but not overconfident. I'm not arrogant, and when it comes to you, I think maybe I should presume even more than I do."

Annie sighed heavily. "I think I'm going to make you walk home."

"Now," Ryan jingled the car keys in front of her, "that would be downright rude of you."

"You think so?"

"Definitely." He was watching her like a hawk.

"Then you're walking home, Pal." Annie angrily snagged the keys out of his hand.

As she went to open her car door, Ryan gently took her hand, and the keys, and held her still. When she looked up into his face, she realized that he was a lot closer to her than she had anticipated. He had leaned over to her side, and their faces were only a few inches apart. He held her burning gaze with one of his own. His look was hard and angry and left no doubt of the fury burning within him. He was ripped, and his expression stated that loud and clear.

"Back off," Annie felt her temper rising rapidly to the boiling point.

"Not a chance." Ryan was quiet but firm.

"You're crowding me."

"Honey, I haven't even begun to crowd you." Ryan's voice sounded barely under control. "When I'm crowding you, you'll know it."

Annie started to struggle to get free from his grip, and Ryan purposely leaned over her, crowding her back into her seat. The air was thick with tension. His blue eyes bore into her until she was about to melt into a puddle. "I don't play games, Annie. I love you. I want you. I want to marry you." Ryan's tone was firm and left absolutely no room for any doubt. "Am I laying my cards on the table clearly enough for you?"

Annie felt like she was drowning. She was totally overwhelmed. She couldn't even attempt to hide the pure shock that flashed across her eyes and then spread like wildfire across her face. Her jaw swung open slightly and the color drained completely from her face. She had suspected all of this. Actually, in her heart she had known it to be true but all she could do was slightly nod at Ryan.

"I can see that my declaration of love thrills you," Ryan mumbled sarcastically.

"It scares me to death," Annie replied in a weak whisper. "It's too soon. It's all too quick. Everything about you and me is just too fast." She closed her eyes for a moment trying to gain control of her spinning emotions. Never before had she felt more vulnerable, afraid or powerless toward another person.

"I agree with you, Annie," Ryan said gently, "it is fast, but on the other hand, it's happened and we need to deal with it. I think it's time you start to deal with all those feeling that you bury deep down. I'm a man who knows what he wants, Annie. I knew it right from the start. And," he released her hands and sighed deeply, "what I want is you."

As Annie slowly pulled away from Ryan all she could do was stare at him. She knew he was very serious about his feelings toward her. It panicked her and she didn't know what to do. Annie earnestly prayed. "Oh God, please, please help me. He is so honest with his feelings and I'm completely afraid to be. I know I ignore my feelings. It's too hard to face them head on. I know I bury them, but it doesn't mean that they're not there. Please, God, help me. I don't even know how to pray about this."

As they rode back to Stony Brook Farm, they were both lost in their thoughts. The ride back was too long, too slow and too silent. Annie couldn't have talked if she had wanted to. She had no words to express the mess that she was feeling inside. She felt like a potato that had just been mashed and was about to be eaten.

Ryan Jones had turned her world upside down. A part of her couldn't wait until he left for Chatfield Hollow and yet another part of her dreaded the separation. She knew that he loved her, and she couldn't deny that it felt wonderful to be loved by a man like Ryan Jones. He never gave himself to anything half heartedly, and that included her. Yet the question that was keeping her awake at night, was, could she ever love him back the way that he deserved to be loved. Could she put the past in the past and go on with the future? She knew she could have a wonderful future with Ryan if the past didn't steal it from her.

Ten

The end of the week came too fast. Before Annie knew it, she was standing in front of Ryan, David, and Gil to say good-bye. She hated good-byes. They were never easy for her and always left a hole in her heart. Ryan had been home schooling David while he was out on the road and she knew that David was anxious to get back to his Christian high school in Tennessee. He missed his friends and all the activities that a normal, healthy sixteen-year-old boy liked to do.

Annie first gave big tearful hugs to David and Gil and then stood awkwardly in front of Ryan twisting her fingers like a nervous schoolgirl. As she gazed up into Ryan's eyes, she immediately noticed that they were flooded in tears. He was looking at her so tenderly that she thought she would melt at his feet. She was disturbed by the way he looked at her and even more disturbed by the way she reacted to him. As she turned her face away from his, and gazed out over the farm fields, she shook her head disgustedly. She didn't have time for this: a relationship, a romance-she didn't even have time for him as a friend. And she thought narrowing her eyes heatedly, especially since a guy like this wasn't likely to stay in the friend category for very long. The only category she wanted him in was off limits, not interested and no trespassing. The problem was, Ryan Jones was definitely within limits, interested in her, and flat out trespassing on her privacy. He was intruding on her life, she thought angrily, and he was a very persistent pain in the backside.

Ryan interrupted her thoughts with a quiet request. "Walk with me for a bit?" Annie nodded and they started off down the scenic dirt road that led around the farm. The road was lined with beautiful maple trees that had fiery red and orange leaves on them. Annie couldn't appreciate their beauty at the moment because her mind was stuck on one thing-Ryan Jones. She was trying hard to convince herself that she didn't want him or need him.

"I've been giving our situation here a lot of thought," Ryan said gently but determinedly.

Annie cast him a quick sideways glance, curious as to where he was going with this conversation. "Somehow that doesn't surprise me," she whispered under her breath.

Ryan heard her and just smiled. "Annie," Ryan continued on like a man on a mission, "I've come to the conclusion that you're afraid to get close to a man. You're afraid to find out what might happen. You're afraid to find out what's on the other side. You like the surface because it's where you feel safe and secure. But," he gently took her hand, "when someone like me comes along, and starts peeling away your layers like an onion, your walls of security start to crumble and it threatens you. Then you do what comes natural to you and that is to run. You need to stop running away, Annie."

In annoyance, Annie withdrew her hand from his. "So when did you get a degree in Psychology? You seem to know so much I guess I should be calling you Dr. Freud now."

Ryan just smiled kindly at her. "I've got more to say."

"Somehow I thought you would."

"You haven't dealt with your feelings about losing your husband, you've just packed them away."

"Well, it works for me," Annie shot back angry. She didn't like her personal life being dissected.

"It doesn't work for you at all," Ryan stated evenly. "You told yourself that for a long time. It doesn't work for you now and it never will."

"Listen," Annie threw her hands on her hips defensively, "I am fine." She blew out a deep breath trying to calm herself down. "I have everything that I've ever dreamed of and more. I am OK."

A knowing smile spread slowly across Ryan's face. "Never try to fool an artistic person Annie." Ryan spoke with annoying calmness and confidence. "We are very much in tune not only with our feelings but with the feelings of those around us. I can see your feelings in your eyes and right now you look like a scared, confused, lost little girl."

Annie glared at him. "I bet my feelings don't tell you that I want to punch you right in the nose."

Ryan's eyebrows rose. "Oh yeah, the anger…I forgot to mention it, but I see that in your eyes too. I don't believe you'd act on your anger."

"Maybe you presume too much."

"I hope I don't." Ryan watched her carefully in case he was wrong.

"I think you should be more careful."

"I thought I was."

"Not nearly careful enough." Annie looked away from him momentarily. She was fuming but she tired hard to control her temper. "Stop treating me like a child. You like to tell me what to do, how to feel and how to act. Did it ever occur to you that I just deal with things differently than you do?"

"That's the point here Annie. You don't deal with things at all. You pack them away, try to ignore them and pray that you'll forget them. You'll never be able to forget things. They will keep coming back to you until you deal with them."

"You think you know everything about me." She stopped and turned to face him directly. "Well you don't."

"I think I know a whole lot more about you than you think. I think that you're so afraid of falling in love, afraid of feeling and afraid that you might meet someone that makes you feel something. I think," Ryan challenged her, "that you're afraid to meet someone that makes you fall in love so deeply that you can't help but love him right back."

Ryan took her hand again and they began slowly walking down the lane. Annie's thoughts were swarming with a variety of emotions. Ryan frightened her because she didn't want to fall in love again. He charmed her, made her feel special and loved, and he seduced her and captivated her. It was too much. She felt like she had a complete and total overload on her heart and mind.

"I want you to know that you are important to me. Everything about you is important to me. I can't stop thinking about you day and night. My mind is on you 24/7."

"Sounds like an obsession," Annie replied in a flippant tone.

"It's the best one that I've ever had," Ryan grinned at her from ear to ear. "Annie," he squeezed her hand, "I know this is meant to be."

"In your dreams," Annie's voice was feisty. She was sick and tired of Ryan telling her what he knew and how to act. As far as she was concerned, Psychology class was now over.

"We'll talk about my dreams another time, Sweetheart," Ryan purred seductively.

Cautiously, Annie withdrew her hand from his. "I don't want to touch you."

"Yes you do," Ryan was quiet but confident.

"Don't tell me what I want and don't want," Annie spat out angrily. "I find that really annoying."

"And I find it really annoying that you don't seem to know, or should I say, that you don't seem willing to admit how you feel about me."

"You really tick me off. You know that?"

Ryan smiled at her. "I believe you mentioned something to that effect before." He took Annie's arm for a second to stop her from walking. He looked at her so lovingly that she couldn't help but look right back at him. "When I touch you, it makes me crazy. I know it makes you crazy too because I can see it in your eyes. There's something between us Annie and it's something that is stronger than I've known in a long time." He took a step closer to her, and put a finger under her chin to lift her eyes up to his. "This feeling between us is too strong to even try to deny. I'm willing to wait until you're ready to accept it. I know in time you will Annie. I know in my heart that it's just a matter of a whole lot of prayer and a bit of time."

Annie's head was spinning. How was she supposed to concentrate on anything when Ryan was standing so close to her? He was close enough for her to smell his enticing aftershave and the natural scent of his skin. It was simply too distractingly close. She shifted and took a step away from him. Ryan immediately closed the distance by taking a step closer to her again. Annie instinctively put a hand up to his chest to stop him and unexpectedly felt the steady rhythm of his heartbeat strong and clear. It mesmerized her and threw her off guard.

With her big brown eyes she looked up into Ryan's face and felt as though she were drowning from all the love and tenderness she saw there. He gently pulled her behind the old gray barn and drew her up to him and kissed her deeply and passionately. The heat between them was instant and the chemistry was flying high. The connection of his touch had her soaring. Annie had always thought of Ryan as being very capable of sweeping a girl off her feet, but knowing it and experiencing it first hand were two very entirely different things. It had been a long time since she had allowed herself to be touched by a man like this. It had also been a long time since she had allowed herself to feel anything. The sensations jolting through her body not only took her by surprise, they nearly knocked her over. She wasn't prepared for it. Annie had known the second she had let Ryan touch her that it had been a mistake. She also knew that she would never get that feeling out of her system. It was explosive, yet extremely gentle. And it was the way a man touched you when he cherished you with all his heart. Ryan brought her to a place that she hadn't been to in a long time and it scared her to death. She had promised herself after her husband's death that she would never go down this road again. It was too painful. Losing her husband had almost destroyed her and she wasn't willing to risk putting herself in that position again. It was too much of him to ask of her and it was definitely too much for her to give. Case closed.

Annie slowly but deliberately pulled back from Ryan. Her head was swimming and her eyes felt out of focus. "I don't think this is a very good idea." Annie's voice came out sounding weak and vulnerable. She wanted to sound sure of herself and confident, but at the moment she wasn't confident or sure of anything.

"I disagree." Ryan pulled her back against himself. "I think it's an extremely good idea."

Annie looked up into Ryan's eyes and felt frightened by the intense, smoldering passion she saw burning brightly there, yet at the same time she couldn't take her eyes off of him. He lowered his gaze to her lips again and then almost regretfully back to her eyes. He was seeking permission from her to continue and she was not about to grant it. They stared at each other, challenge meeting challenge. It was more than a simple contest; it was a battle for the rights to her heart and her life. Annie wasn't ready to turn that over yet. His gaze dropped to her lips again and he dipped his head down a fraction of an inch closer to her. She knew she was about to be kissed again and she also knew that she couldn't let that happen. She knew that if she let him kiss her again, it would be over for her. She would stay in his arms and become his, and she wasn't ready to belong to any man quite yet. Annie slowly pushed away.

Ryan looked at her through disappointed, puzzled eyes. "Don't be afraid Annie. You can trust me."

Annie slowly shook her head. "I'm not ready for this. And, for the record, I am very much afraid of you. You scare me to death. You have quickly worked your way into areas of my heart that I vowed no man would ever get close to again. I don't know exactly when it happened, but you're there, and it frightens me more than I can say."

Annie paused and let out a loud troubled sigh. "I'm asking for time, Ryan. I need time to figure this all out. I need time to think and pray about this."

"You think too much."

She took another step back from him to put some much-needed distance between them. "Thinking about things has kept me alive."

Ryan looked at her with an expression that held both love and frustration. "You're just starting to feel alive for the first time in years, Annie. You know I'm right."

Ryan felt more shaken on the inside than he appeared on the outside. He wanted Annie permanently in his life. He had told her that. He smiled. He was never one to beat around the bush, but as he watched her, he knew she was far from being ready. She was frightened and she was right. He did need to give her time to deal with her fears. He knew this was going to be one of the toughest battles that he had ever fought. The only way he'd make it through was by prayer, and, Ryan smiled again, a whole lot of it.

"Walk back to the bus with me?" Ryan asked in a choked up voice. Annie nodded and they slowly began to walk back toward the others. "I'm going to call you every day."

Annie looked startled. "Ryan, that's too much! You can't do that."

Ryan smiled impishly at her and then softly whispered, "OK, every other day." As they approached the bus, he turned and gave her a big hug and then softly brushed a kiss across her cheek. As he boarded the bus, Annie felt as though she were going to be sick. She wanted him to go, really needed him to go, yet something deep inside her screamed not to ever let him go.

Annie took Amy's hand and the two of them went over to sit on the back porch steps while their new family got ready to leave. After about five minutes, the bus still hadn't moved. Gil and David reappeared and ran quickly by Annie and Amy in the direction of the red barn. Ryan flew out of the bus next and headed toward the house.

"Misplaced the keys..."Ryan mumbled, sounding embarrassed as he dashed up the steps and into the house.

"Mom," Amy got up quickly, "we should help them look for their keys.

Annie smiled mischievously at her daughter. Amy studied her mom with a surprised expression on her face. "Mom, you didn't!"

A low giggle escaped from Annie's mouth, as she dangling the missing keys in front of her daughter. "Mom, you're terrible!" The expression on Amy's face told her mother that she totally approved of her prank.

"I couldn't help it." Annie giggled again. "When Ryan was hugging me good bye, his keys were practically falling out of his back pocket. They weren't hard to lift."

Mother and daughter laughed again, and then Amy looked at her mom expectantly. "What's our plan?"

"Well, Sweetie, we really do have several options here." They both laughed again. "You know, I've always wondered what it would be like to drive one of those great big tour buses."

"You're kidding!" Amy exploded excitedly. "Do you think that you could?"

Annie nodded and she and Amy got up and slowly started walking toward the tour bus. "I think so, Honey. Remember, I grew up on this farm driving Grandpa's tractors. A bus can't be that different from a big farm tractor."

The bus thieves quickly made their way on board the bus and then locked the door behind them. Annie slid into the driver's seat and impressively studied the control panel before her. "This sure is a lot nicer than Grandpa's tractors!"

Annie shoved the key into the ignition and the big bus roared to life. Amy cheered excitedly. Annie put her right hand on the stick shift and her left foot down on the clutch. She eased the bus into first gear and it instantly, slowly started creeping forward.

A moment later, David and Gil, who must have heard the bus start up, came walking out of the barn. They stared at the bus, with obvious concern running across their faces. Amy laughed. "Mom, they think that someone is trying to steal their bus! HA!" Amy roared with laughter again.

Annie had to laugh at the sight of big Gil, with his hands placed determined on his hips. He didn't like anyone messing with his bus. Annie steered the front of the bus slowly toward him, and when she got close enough, she laid a heavy hand on the loud bus horn. David and Gil jumped about a mile straight up in the air. As they regained their senses, and identified the bus thieves, their mouths dropped open and they stood there with a look of sheer disbelief on their trusting faces. Annie blew the horn again and they ran out of the way of the slow moving bus.

A few seconds later, Ryan casually came out of the house, thinking that someone had found the keys. When he saw David and Gil plastered up against the side of the red barn, he quickly looked back at the bus with alarm.

Annie blew the horn again and then she and Amy gave a great big spunky wave to Ryan. He stared at Annie behind the wheel of his bus as if she were a Martian that had just landed from space. He couldn't believe it. He looked frozen in place until Annie laid on the horn again. That snapped him out of his trance and he turned and looked at Gil with a grin that was filled with amusement. The war had just been declared.

"Amy?" Annie asked her daughter quickly, "are David's super soaker's still back there?

"Mom, that would be cruel!"

Annie glanced at her daughter quickly. "Yes dear, I know. It will be just a little something for them to remember us by. Go load them up in the buses kitchen sink."

The three men watched in amusement as the bus made its way down the long dirt road and around a barn. When Annie pulled the bus up directly behind one of the large red barns, she turned off the engine and went back to help Amy load their weapons. When they were full, the mother/daughter SWAT team crept to one of the large tinted black windows and opened it just a few inches. They didn't say anything, but waited patiently for their three victims to come closer to the bus. It didn't take very long. Ryan approached the bus immediately, his face glowing with laughter.

"Annie," his voice was filled with delight, "that was very, very funny of you. You lifted my keys. Why you little thief!"

Annie planned her moment carefully. Just as Ryan jumped up to peak inside the tinted window, she let her super soaker rip. His face, hair, and chest were instantly plastered with water. David and Gil were just behind Ryan and Amy skillfully doused them.

"OK, Ladies," Ryan addressed the bus sternly, keeping a careful distance from the tinted window that had ambushed him, "you've had your fun, now unlock the door."

Annie and Amy went to another tinted window and whipped it open quickly. Annie took aim at Ryan again, while Amy concentrated most of her firepower on David. The men ran away quickly, but the SWAT team still managed to soak their back pretty well.

"This is war!" David waved his hands in the air at the bus. The Annie and Amy laughed at the sight.

"Is he just realizing that now, mom?" Amy laughed at David's antics.

"I think so," Annie laughed. "Nothing like surprising the enemy."

Safely out of range, the men regrouped and planned their attack. Annie and Amy watched them curiously, as they leaned against the white board fence planning and plotting.

As the three men walked away from the fence, Annie watched them carefully. When their destination hit them, she gasped. "Oh no! I left the house unlocked."

Amy stared at her mother in semi horror. "Mom, what are we going to do? We really did spring this on them."

Annie nodded and smiled. "And now it's time for us to reap what we've sown." Annie paused for a minute and then glanced over at her daughter. Snapping her fingers together, she said excitedly, "Am, we really should sneak off the bus while they're in the house. Then maybe we won't have to reap what we've sown quite so soon!"

"What do you think they're up to?" Amy asked curiously.

Annie thought for a minute, and then her eyes went wide with the realization of what they were probably doing. "The water balloons in the kitchen cabinet…"

"The ones we bought for youth group?"

Annie ran a hand through her short brown hair. "Those would be the ones."

"There are a lot of them!"

"Yeah," Annie nodded thoughtfully. "Ryan noticed them in the cabinet when he was looking for a pen and paper the other day. He was pretty excited about them. That's got to be what he's up to." Annie paused again thoughtfully, planning and scheming in her mind. "You know, we'd better refill our super soakers before we get off the bus."

Amy agreed, and the two of them went back to the small kitchen and began their job. They refilled their guns and quickly exited the bus. Annie shut the bus door, and then locked it behind her. Amy gave her a quizzical look.

"If they push against the door," Annie smiled at her daughter, "I want them to see that it's still locked. I want them to think that we're still inside the bus."

Amy smiled approvingly at her mom. "Good one."

They rapidly made their way to the old gray barn a few hundred feet away. They were careful to stay directly behind the red barn so they were completely out of sight from the kitchen window. When they made it safely to the back of the gray barn, they sat down on the grass and waited.

"Honey," Annie touched her daughter's arm, "we're going to get wet. You know that, don't you?"

Amy laughed quietly. "I know mom. I don't care. This is the most fun that we've had in a long time."

Annie leaned over and hugged her daughter. "I love you, Am."

"I love you too, mom."

They hugged again, and then the two of them crept to the end of the barn to spy on what was happening. The three men stood bravely next to the side of the bus, with a five gallon bucket filled to the top with water balloons.

"Mom," Amy slid around to the back of the barn again, "how on earth did they fill them all up so quickly?"

Annie laughed. "Something tells me that they're professionals at this, Dear. I bet they divided up and used the kitchen sinks as well as the bathroom sinks. It's the only way they could have loaded that bucket so quickly."

They popped their heads around the corner of the barn again and were near hysterics watching as the men made all kinds of threatening remarks at the empty bus. It was almost too much! A low giggle escaped Amy's mouth. It was just loud enough for the enemy to hear it. Immediately a battle cry arouse from David.

"Dad! They're behind the gray barn! Charge!" David and Gil instantly took off running toward the gray barn.

"Mom! What to we do?" Amy was beginning to panic.

"Stand your ground soldier! This is the best cover we've got. When they get close enough to us, let 'em have it."

They did just that for the next ten minutes. Annie and Amy had an all out water fight with David and Gil. Annie was so busy defending her turf, that she didn't hear Ryan slowly approaching from the other side of the barn. As David and Gil retreated, out of ammo, the girls laid their near empty super soakers on the ground. As Annie leaned against the back of the barn, feeling exhausted, she surveyed the damage. Amy had taken a few direct hits to her shoulder and her jeans. Annie looked down at herself and was surprised. "Am, can you believe it? I didn't get hit once!"

Annie heard a low growl from Ranger, and turned to see Ryan quickly coming toward her. She jumped up to run, but Ryan swiftly moved in front of her, blocking her emergency exit path. He slowly began pushing her back, deep into the corner of the barn's extension, smiling at her mischievously the entire time. As Annie looked back at him, she noticed that he had two good-sized water balloons in his hands. He raised one slightly, grinning at Annie shamelessly.

"You know," Annie's voice was quick, with just a hint of desperation in it, "you really don't need to get me with those. We can call a truce right now."

Ryan's charming grin only broadened. "Oh," he stated in a satisfied tone, "I just love it when the prisoner begs for mercy!" Ryan laughed loudly, and the sound echoed off the corners of the barn extension. "Annie, we had a truce. You broke it." Another loud laugh escaped his lips and he stood there grinning at her triumphantly. "You," he eyed her steadily, "pick pocketed my keys from me when I gave you a hug good-bye."

Annie couldn't contain her laughter. It slowly began to bubble up and spill out. She bit her bottom lip to try to restrain it.

"And," Ryan leaned down a little, to look her squarely in the eye, "you shanghaied our bus!" He let out a loud laugh. "Where did you ever learn to drive a bus?"

"I grew up on the farm here," Annie replied in a matter-of-fact way. "During harvest season, things got very busy. We all had to pitch in. I started driving the tractor as soon as my feet could touch the pedals."

Ryan smiled at her proudly. "I bet you were good at it too."

Annie smiled at him. As they talked she had been looking for a way to escape. Unfortunately, Ryan had pushed her back into the barn extension so far that it seemed impossible to get around him.

Ryan read her mind and howled with laughter. "Now, Annie, "he acted as though he were in shock, "you don't seriously think that you can escape from me. Do you? There is no way past me. You're in jail here, Babe, and I can tell you right now that you aren't going to receive a pardon!" He sounded so cocky and victorious, and to Annie's regret, she knew that he was right.

Slowly, almost in a torturing way, Ryan lifted one large water balloon in the air. He dangled it above her brunette head for a moment before he let it come crashing down on her head. Annie screamed and wiped the water from her face. Ryan just stared at her, smiling unashamedly. The smug satisfaction of tasting his revenge was clearly marked on his face.

He leaned down toward her again, and said in a teasing, light, playful tone, "I'm sorry, Honey, but you really did deserve that."

Annie was a good sport. She smiled back at him, and then turned her attention to the other water balloon in his hand. "And," she asked eyeing the balloon wearily, "do I deserve that one too?"

Ryan smiled charmingly and then nodded his head. "Absolutely." As he looked directly into her brown eyes, in a quick unpredicted moment, he swung the water balloon behind him dousing Amy in the side. Amy screamed, and took off running away from them with Ranger and Scout following at her heels. Ryan turned his attention back to a giggling Annie.

"Good shot." She was very impressed. "How did you do that?"

"I have good peripheral vision." He leaned closer to her. "Besides, I had to do something to get rid of Amy so I could be alone with you."

Annie's eyes instantly widened. "I don't think you really believe me." Ryan's tone was quiet but earnest.

"Believe you?" Annie asked in a wobbly voice.

"Yes." Ryan studied her closely. "I don't think you have any idea how much I truly love you." He paused for a moment and then exhaled loudly. "I fell in love with you the moment I saw you in the concert hall."

Annie shook her head adamantly. "Ryan," her voice was firm, "I've been thinking about this too. And you know what? The truth suddenly dawned on me. You see, you think that you're in love with me, but, you're really not."

A grin started tugging at the corners of Ryan's mouth and gradually spread across his face. He raised questioning eyebrows at her. "Oh, no?"

"No," Annie answered resolutely.

"You don't think that I know my own heart?"

Annie shook her head determinedly. "I think that this has been an emotional roller coaster for both of us. I think you've fallen in love with me the same way that a soldier falls in love with a nurse that has saved his life. It's not love," Annie's voice was very practical, "it's something else."

Ryan didn't appear the least bit discouraged by Annie's statement at all. He closed his eyes for a moment, dropping his head a bit, and smiling broadly. Annie looked up at his perfectly charming smile and had to close her own eyes for a minute in hopes of blocking this man of out her mind. At that moment, Ryan leaned down and brushed a soft kiss across Annie's check. Her eyes immediately flew open and she stared at Ryan in alarm.

He stepped back from her a little to give them both some much-needed space. "Annie," he said in a tender, confident voice, "I do love you." He prayed that she would see it was true. "I know that for sure. But," he eyed her seriously, "I am going to pray for you, every day, that God will reveal my honest, loving, good, Christian intentions toward you. I am going to pray for your heart to be healed. Your heart needs to be healed from your Ryan's death," he spoke kindly in an understanding way. "Until it truly is, I know you can never enter into a godly, loving relationship."

As Ryan's words hit Annie, she slumped back against the barn, feeling frustrated and defeated. She glanced up at him with tearful eyes. "Ryan," her tone was empty and hopeless, "I don't know where my heart is. My heart and my head seem to be in two different places. I am so confused and in so much pain. Tell me," she asked desperately, "when does the pain really go away? This knife slicing pain rips you apart...when will it go away?" Annie closed her eyes for a minute to gather her strength. She willed herself to continue. "I feel as though I'm on a sailboat out in the middle of the ocean. My boat is slowly taking on water and there is no land in sight. I am trying furiously to bail the water out of my boat, yet the water just keeps pouring in." Annie's voice grew tight. "It's like," she said clenching her fists together, "I know that my boat is going down. I know that I'm sinking. It's only a matter of time."

"Annie," Ryan's voice was choked up, "you need to get off your sinking ship. You've got to let God lift you up onto His solid rock." He took her hands and squeezed them encouragingly. "Take it from a guy who's been there Honey. God is the only one that can get you through this. Others can help you and comfort you. They can listen to you, pray for you, and just be there for you. But," he squeezed her hands again, "God is the only one that can really heal your heart. No one else can, just God alone."

Ryan took Annie and cradled her tenderly in a loving embrace. Softly he whispered in her ear. "Honey, I'll be waiting for you until your heart is healed. Let God heal you, Annie. It's the only way you can get over such deep, heart-wrenching pain."

Ryan kissed her on her wet forehead, and then stepped back from her. "Well, I should be hitting the road now. I don't want to go, but I've got to." He gently took her hand. "Are you going to be alright?" Annie nodded. She was too choked up to say anything.

"Oh," Ryan smiled at her, "I need the bus keys back. It's time you handed them over, you little thief!"

As Annie struggled to pull them from her wet pocket, Ryan leaned over her. He spoke in words that were far too serious for her. "If you don't hand the keys back now, I'm going to have to kiss you long and passionately until you do."

Annie stiffened and then mechanically yanked the keys out of her pocket. As she handed them to Ryan, he took the keys, and her hand, and led her back to the bus. "You have to come say good-bye again to David and Gil."

Annie nodded and looked over to see David, Gil and Amy sitting on the white board fence. Humor was written all over their faces.

"So," David teased, "I see that you have captured your prisoner and tortured her well!"

Ryan and Annie laughed. "You bet!" Ryan winked at Annie.

They said a tearful good-bye again, and then Annie and Amy watched as the big silver, maroon and black tour bus slowly made it's way down the dirt country lane away from the farm. Annie stood there, watching the road long after the bus was out of sight. Her heart was filled with so many mixed emotions that she felt completely drained and a bit numb. Ranger and Scout came up to her side and she patted the dogs lovingly. She was grateful for the two large shepherds. They had a keen sense of knowing when she needed them.

Annie closed her eyes and silently sent a prayer heavenward. "Oh Lord, I'm feeling so mixed up right now. Please help me to look to you. Help me to lean on you to get me through this. Ryan Jones has brought back a spark to this dead heart of mine. I want to love again, but I'm so afraid to let anyone get close to me again. Please Father, please help me."

Eleven

As Annie and Bob walked around the farm they talked easily with one another as best friends often do. Bob was Annie's older brother and she thought the world of him. Annie trusted Bob's advice and she trusted him with her secrets like no other person she knew. Things were safe with Bob. He didn't talk to others about the things she confided in him. He seemed to have an uncanny sense of how far to push her, when to stop giving advice, and when she simply needed a great big hug.

Bob lived on a small island off the coast of Maine with his wife Jude and their little daughter Heidi. Every time he came down to Boston on business, he would drop by the farm for a day or two to catch up with Annie and the kids. Annie always looked forward to their visits.

"So," Bob asked in his normal laid-back style, "tell me about the celebrity. I loved all the emails that you sent over the past few weeks, but I'll have to admit, Annie, you were a little vague at times when you answered my questions."

Annie smiled at Bob. He knew her far too well
for her to even try to pull one over on him. She was
vague about Ryan Jones because she didn't know
what to tell Bob. If she said too much, she might
end up confessing something she didn't want to.

"Well," Annie tried to play it casual, "he's a nice
guy. It's amazing how much he does look like my
Ryan. It kind of threw me at first, but as I got to
know him better, I began to see plenty of differences to help separate the two."

Bob smiled at her with a glimmer of humor in
his eye. He knew that Annie was holding out on
him. He wondered how much of the formalities
he'd have to listen to before she broke down and
talked to him straight. Ranger trotted up beside
him, and he scratched the big dog behind the ears
as he curiously glanced at his little sister.

"What?" Annie asked guardedly.

Bob laughed loudly and she enjoyed the sound of
it. Bob was a big stocky guy, over six feet tall, broad
as a linebacker, and had the heart of a teddy bear.
When she looked up into his baby face, with his
neatly trimmed brown hair, and big brown eyes, she
could never stay angry or distant from him for long.

"I'm going to play it straight with you Sis," Bob
said good-naturedly. "You told me a lot of things
about Ryan Jones, but what I'm more interested in
are the things you haven't said." He winked at her.

"You know, like all those little things you so carefully avoided mentioning in your emails."

"Such as?" Annie asked defensively.

"Such as, why you have rented so much space in your heart and your head to a man that you claim is just a good friend. From what you've said, it seems like the man doesn't want to be a renter but a permanent tenant." Bob raised his eyebrows at Annie questioningly. "Care to expand your definition of your relationship with the celebrity? Or, are you going to make me drag it out of you?"

"I don't have a relationship with Ryan," Annie replied heatedly.

Bob just laughed. "You know, Ann, I never figured you for the type to get star struck over some good looking celebrity guy. It's not your style."

"I am not star-struck." Annie was getting angry.

Bob put his arm around his sister and gave her a loving embrace. "Talk to me, Annie. Don't freeze me out. I want to help you through this."

Annie sighed heavily. "Oh, Bob," her voice was tight, "I think you may be right."

Bob smiled at her. "I'm your older, wiser brother. I'm always right." Annie went to jab him in the ribs, but he evaded her. "So tell me, for the record, what am I right about this time?"

"Ryan Jones has marched into my well ordered, predictable world, and turned it upside down."

Annie paused and ran a hand nervously through her hair. "He has a control over me, and a power over my emotions - and I don't like it! I can't seem to help myself around him. I'm not a star struck teenager. I am not one to be run by my emotions and this whole thing just ticks me off!"

Bob smiled at her kindly. "I didn't need the news flash on that Sis. I can see the man has affected you."

"I just don't need this in my life right now. Not now," Annie sighed frustrated, "and not ever again."

"So," Bob asked gently, "you think about this singer guy a lot?"

Annie started to cry. She hated feeling out of control and right now she felt like her life had been hit by a tornado. Bob put a loving arm around her but stayed quiet. He knew that Annie would talk when she was ready.

"Bob," Annie was irritated, "I think about Ryan Jones almost all the time. I even dream about him. Is that crazy, or what?"

Bob smiled tenderly at his little sister. "You're sunk, Ann. You don't even know it yet, but you are. It will be interesting to see how long it takes for you to realize that you are in love with this guy."

"I am not!" Annie grew intensely adamant. "You have got to be kidding. In love…."

"Yes," Bob reached down to toss a stick to Ranger, "I'd say that you're head over heels in love.

You'll figure it out sooner or later. But," Bob smiled down at his little sister almost obnoxiously, "knowing you, it will be later. You tend to be a bit slow on these things. Your first instinct is to go the denial route."

"Denial route, my foot. I am not in denial. Just shut up Bob."

"Oh...now this is extremely interesting." Bob stopped walking and turned to face his sister directly. "The only time you ever tell me to shut up is when I'm right. So I am right! I don't know why I ever doubt myself. I am always right."

Bob put a finger under Annie's chin, and slowly raised her face so their eyes met. "I am right about this. Aren't I?"

"Bob," Annie looked at him angrily, "stop chewing on me. You think you've got things pegged, but you don't."

"Then talk to me," Bob asked in a reasonable tone.

"I'm not sure I can," Annie replied honestly. "I'm still trying to figure it all out myself."

"Tell me what you've come up with so far."

Annie shook her head slightly and sighed loudly. "I'm a mess."

"Uh, I already figured that one out."

Annie had to laugh. Bob always saw the lighter side of things and helped bring her to the middle.

He was good at helping her to balance things out. "OK," she nodded thoughtfully, "we're just all wrong for each other. He travels the world singing, and I like to stay home. He thrives on change, where I cling to my nice little neat routine. He sings beautifully," Annie laughed, "and I can't hold a note. You know how I've always had my own range."

"You've always been a little tone deaf," Bob teased, "but I don't see what that has to do with anything, unless you're planning on performing with him on stage."

"No way!" Annie answered quickly. "I'd rather die a thousand deaths!"

"OK. So back to the real issues." Bob looked over at his sister sympathetically. "You may be a little resistant to what I have to say." Bob paused and sighed loudly. "Aw shoot, Annie, you're not going to like what I have to say, but I have always been honest with you, and I'm not about to change that now."

"Go on," she moaned cautiously.

"I think that you're trying so hard not to fall in love with Ryan Jones, that you're completely blinded to the fact that you already are."

"You're right," Annie narrowed her eyes at her brother, "not only do I not like what you've said, I completely and totally disagree with it. You're ridiculous."

Bob shook his head sadly. "Annie, you have always guarded your heart so closely. You don't even see this. I had to be the one to tell you that you were falling in love with Ryan Smith. Remember?"

"That was completely different and has no bearing on this at all."

"You never saw it then and you don't see it now." Bob paused thoughtfully. "You have always been kind of weird that way."

"I have not," Annie stated unyieldingly.

Bob put a firm hand on Annie's shoulder. "You are falling in love with him Kid, and the sooner you accept it, the sooner you can really move on with your life."

"I'm not in love." Annie rubbed Scout's soft ears. "I think I may be going through a mid life crisis, or quite possibly a nervous breakdown. It's not love."

Bob laughed. Annie reacted exactly how he thought she would. "Listen," he put his arm around her, "what are you so afraid of?"

"I'm not afraid of anything!" Annie pulled away from him.

"Annie," Bob laughed loudly, "you're afraid of everything! And right now, you're completely afraid of falling in love again."

Annie glared at Bob. She didn't know what to say, so she stayed quiet.

"Annie," Bob put his arm back around her, "give it over to God. He wants you to be happy. He has given you a gift in Ryan Jones. Don't throw it away."

"I am completely defenseless against him," Annie whimpered

"Yeah," Bob laughed again, "and I bet that really grinds at you. You're such a control freak. You have to be in control of everything."

"I am not a control freak."

"Yeah, you are."

"Shut up Bob."

Bob stood back and smiled at her. "See, you're telling me to shut up again. I guess that means that I'm right about this too. Man," his tone became exaggerated, "being right two times in one day is almost more than a guy can take."

"If you weren't my brother, I'd clobber you."

"Shoot, Annie," Bob's face swam in amusement, "you've been saying that for years. Do you really think that I take that threat seriously?"

A loud troubled sigh escaped Annie's lips. "How can I be in love with two men at the same time? If I was, I'd be acting unfaithful and unfair to both of them. I need to have only one man in my heart." She was in agony. "What if I had met Ryan Jones before I met Ryan Smith. Would I have married him instead? What if we were all in college together, and they were standing side by side.

Which one would I choose? How can I ever choose between them? Even now that my Ryan is gone, I still feel like I'm being forced to choose between them, and you know what? I can't.

"You're going to drive yourself crazy," Bob whispered gently.

"Yeah, maybe so, but these are questions that are keeping me awake at night."

"You can't live your life with the 'What if's'. You've got to keep to what you know is true. Stay with the facts Annie and you'll do better."

"But my head..." Annie felt helpless.

"It's always been a problem for you. You tend to think too much and not listen to the Lord and your heart. You need to listen to your heart."

"You sound like a cheap greeting card," Annie mumbled. "It is incredibly irritating. Stop it."

"But I'm right." Bob smirked at her confidently.

"Yes," Annie sighed exasperatedly. "And that annoys me even more!"

Twelve

$\mathscr{R}$yan was good to his word and phoned Annie faithfully every few days. Annie hated to admit it, even to herself, how much she really looked forward to Ryan's phone calls. Through the daily phone conversations, their friendship deepened and grew.

One evening on the phone Ryan suggested to Annie that they start doing a weekly devotion together. "I know a really great book," he told her enthusiastically, "I'll send it along to you in the mail." Annie eagerly agreed.

Two days later a package arrived by Fed Ex from Ryan. Inside were a bunch of items along with a devotional book. As soon as Annie picked the book up, she felt her back stiffen and her defenses go up. The title screamed out at her loud and clear. Helping You Deal With The Loss Of A Loved One. She instantly dropped the book down on the counter as if it had burned her. She stared at the title angrily.

"Just what does he think!" Annie's fists were balled at her sides and she began to pace back and forth in the kitchen. She was fuming. "Does he think he can judge how I'm dealing with the death of my husband? How in the world am I supposed to deal with it anyways?"

Ranger and Scout stared at Annie intently. They were alert, listening to her ranting and raving, but they also looked like they didn't have a clue as to what to do about it. Annie shook her head sadly at the dogs and knelt down to stroke their soft tan fur. They had been through a lot with her and she appreciated their loyal loving support.

As Annie glared back at the book on the counter, her own words began to convict her. "Dealing with Ryan's death..." She knew, deep down, that not only had she not dealt with it well, she really hadn't dealt with it at all. It was too painful and the hurt went too deep.

She went over to one of her wooden, ladder back kitchen chairs, pulled it from the table and slumped down in it. She covered her face with her hands as the true realization of that fact hit her hard. She hadn't dealt with Ryan's death and because of that she really hadn't helped her kids deal with the loss of their father. She had locked the door closed on that part of her life and vowed to never open it again.

Annie laid her head on the kitchen table and wept. So much pain and hurt that she had held onto since

Ryan's death came pouring out through her tears. Her body shook violently as the tears streamed out in torrents. She felt angry with Ryan for dying and guilty that she felt angry with him. She had always envisioned them having a long happy life together, and that little phrase 'till death do us part' wouldn't even be considered until they were at least one hundred years old. That was the minimum.

Their love had been such a special kind of love. It grew steadily deeper with each passing year. She had never felt more loved and cherished in her entire life. Dealing with the death of Ryan, really dealing with it, would mean she would have to accept the fact that she wasn't ever going to grow old with him, and that the one true love of her life was gone.

The pain continued to hit her fast and hard. She fought for each breath as her tears threatened to choke her like a noose. The realization of the truth left her feeling cold, lonely and empty inside. He was gone. He was never coming back.

Annie missed her husband so much. She found it was the little things that she missed the most about him. She missed his warm glowing smile, the sound of his laughter and his great big tender bear hugs. She missed their quiet talks on the back porch and their rowdy playful teasing times together. She missed the way he would look at her as if she were the most beautiful woman in the world. He made her feel so special, so cherished, and like she was his most prized treasure. He simply made her feel.... While she went racing through life, worrying about situations, bills, and their kids, it was Ryan who knew how to slow her world down. He'd make her stop and notice things in life, like the great beauty around them, how much their kids loved them, and how fortunate they were to have each other. He had a knack for pointing out the things in life that were the most important, and the most easy to take for granted. He slowed her down and helped her to focus her heart and mind on the Lord.

Annie longed for Ryan and all the things they had together. She felt a deep pain in her heart as she accepted the fact that they could never share life together again. "Could you share it with someone else?" A voice that was sudden and loud inside her seemed to ask this question. Annie immediately felt guilty. How could she ever think of dating or getting remarried again? Just the thought of it filled her with guilt and made her feel unfaithful to her late husband. "I think I would always feel like I were cheating on him and doing something terribly wrong," Annie's soft words floated out to the void of the kitchen. "We were such a great team and respected and trusted each other completely, and in every way." Annie shook her head slowly and ran a hand through her hair.

As Annie began to break down in tears again, she let her head fall into her hands and quietly began to pray. "Oh God," her voice was desperate and completely void of hope, "Ryan Jones is right. I'm not dealing with the death of my husband well." Her voice choked up and she paused to try to catch her breath. "Father, when you brought Ryan into my life, it was the best thing that ever happened to me besides you. Ryan was everything that I ever dreamed of in a man and so much more. He treated me like a princess, and I thought of him as my prince charming. I loved him so much and still do." Annie paused, fighting back the emotions that threaten to bury her. "Please God, I need your help to get through this. I want to have a godly man around to love again, but even at the thought of it I feel as though I've sinned. I feel like I'm having an affair and I'm trying to hide it from my Ryan." Annie sobbed loudly. "Lord, I've asked you to help me deal with the hurt and the pain of losing Ryan, but dear Father, help me to deal with the guilt as well. Please make my heart whole again and make my children whole again. Help me to help them through this and teach them how to deal with the death of their dad and not bury it."

As Annie ended her prayer, she felt completely drained and exhausted, yet deep down in her heart; she felt a sense of peace and hope that hadn't been there before. She couldn't remember the last time she had felt peace or hope in her heart. It had been so long it was like a distant memory. Her problems were now in the hands of her Heavenly Father. Annie felt as though a great weight had been lifted off her. She sat quietly for a few minutes, bathing in the new freedom and peace she was experiencing.

As Annie remembered the box that Ryan had sent, she got up and went over to the kitchen counter and picked it up. She spied a large yellow envelope and pulled it out of the box quickly. She brought it back to the table and sat down in her chair again. As she opened the envelope, she pulled out two pictures and a letter. Annie carefully studied the pictures and soon a loving smile spread across her face. The first photo was a group shot of Ryan and his kids. Even the family dog had made it into the picture. His name was Banjo and he was a beautiful Golden Lab, with a red handkerchief tied around his neck. The picture was taken at their ranch in Chatfield Hollow and a white barn, with breath taking mountains were in the background. Annie studied the friendly picture a moment longer and then put it down and picked up the other photo.

This photo was a professional picture of the contemporary Christian singer Ryan Jones. Ryan was sitting casually at his black piano and smiling that charming smile that makes you go weak in the knees. Even his blue eyes had a hint of laughter behind them. It was a great shot of him and Annie continued to smile at it lovingly.

As she flipped the picture over, she noticed a message on the other side.

"To Annie,

I'm so thankful that the Lord brought you into my life. You have captured my heart, my thoughts, and my prayers. God Bless,

Love,

Ryan

Annie read the message again, and than flipped the picture back over to look at Ryan. Something in her heart stirred, and for the first time, Annie felt that she could finally admit to herself that she cared for this loving man, gorgeous as he was, just slightly more than a friend. Annie smiled as laughter escaped her lips. "Yeah," she studied the picture of Ryan, "just slightly more then a friend."

Annie took the envelope and pulled out a white piece of stationery paper. The paper had a solid navy line bordering it and inside it was Ryan's block style handwriting. She read the words anxiously.

Dear Annie, (or should I call you psycho-wheelchair driver, pick pocket thief, bus thief, or super soaker expert! I guess I'll stick to Annie because it's such a pretty name.)

I've enclosed the devotional book that I mentioned on the phone, along with a few photos. If you don't care for my selection of devotional materials, feel free to pick out something else. The book is not as important as the time we spend together growing closer to each other and the Lord.

You're always in my thoughts and prayers,

Love,

Ryan

Annie read the letter again and then put it back into the envelope. "He is so open Father," Annie prayed silently. "He doesn't even mind if I pick out the devotional book…" Annie let her thoughts trail off for a minute. "But," she whispered tilting her head a bit, "this book is perfect for us. I think it's exactly what we need and exactly what we need to go through with each other and with you."

Thirteen

When Ryan called the next day, he immediately inquired as to whether or not Annie had received the package he sent her. "Yes," Annie smiled into the phone, "I love the photos you sent me. They're great! The mountains that you live around look beautiful."

"They are! You'll see them for yourself when you come down at Christmastime."

"Uh, Ryan, I didn't say that we were coming for Christmas for sure. I said that we would think about."

"You're going to think about it and then you're going to come." Ryan was quite sure of himself. "I can't wait to see you at Christmas! I miss you so much."

"I miss you too," Annie whispered softly.

The silence on the other end of the phone was deafening. Slowly, in a voice filled with unmistakable hope, Ryan asked cautiously, "Do you really Annie? Do you really miss me?"

Annie cleared her throat nervously. "Yes."

There was another pause and then Ryan asked hesitantly, "Has there been some sort of change Annie?"

Annie sighed heavily into the phone. "Yes," she answered in a voice that was just above a whisper.

There was another pause and Annie could almost picture the wheels spinning in Ryan's mind. "Anything that you want to talk about?"

Annie could hear the hope mounting in his voice and she laughed nervously. "Not yet, but sometime soon. God is just really doing a work in my heart."

"Healing?" Ryan asked lovingly.

"Yes," Annie admitted slowly. "I'm just having trouble pulling all my thoughts together on this one. The way some things are...words are not adequate to express how I feel. Especially," Annie's voice began pained, "about my Ryan. I have never been able to find the right words to express how I feel about losing him. And," Annie pushed herself to go on, "I finally realized why. There are no words that can possibly express how I feel about losing him. They simply don't exist. It's too deep."

"Just remember," Ryan said lovingly, "that if you really place your life in God's hands, then you don't need to be afraid of where he's leading you. He will take care of you."

Annie laughed. She couldn't help it. "And you think God is leading me to you!"

Ryan laughed loudly. "Annie, I've known that for a while now. I've simply been waiting, not so patiently, for God to show it to you. I've been down on my knees a lot about his one."

"You think you know so much."

"I'll tell you one thing that I do know," Ryan admitted smugly, "you're not nearly as tough as you'd like people to think that you are."

Annie quietly made a snide comment, that Ryan caught just enough of to realize that he'd just been trashed. He laughed loudly. This woman was going to keep him on his toes.

"You want to know something else?" Ryan asked with a calm self-assurance.

"Not really, but somehow I don't think that's going to stop you. You seem to be on sort of a roll here."

"I knew you'd want to know," Ryan teased her. "Annie, you don't ever have to accept my love. That is strictly your choice. But," his voice was growing thick with intensity, "there is absolutely nothing you can do to stop my love for you. It only grows deeper every day. You can try to walk away from it, or deny it exists, but if you're honest with yourself, and open your heart up just a little, you'll see it there."

Annie sighed heavily. She wasn't ready to talk about this. "You know what? Let's change the subject. Let's talk about some thing light, like the weather."

Ryan laughed. "OK. How's your weather?"

"Fine," Annie answered nonchalantly.

"Great. Mine is too. By the way, did you get the book that I sent you?"

"I thought we were talking about the weather."

"We were. We finished. Did you get the book?" Annie laughed. "You're a persistent little mosquito, aren't you?"

"You bet!" Ryan didn't take offense in the least. "So, what did you think about the book?"

Annie laughed loudly as she thought of her first response to it.

"What?" Ryan asked anxiously. "If you don't like it, we can pick out something else."

"No, it's fine."

"Are you sure?" Ryan asked hesitantly.

"Yes, yes, it's perfect. When I first saw it, I got a little angry at the title of the book." She paused searching for the right words. "Ryan, you and this book are making me face a lot of tough issues." Annie sighed and then said quietly, "Well, actually one really tough issue."

"I know," Ryan was filled with compassion. "Do you think that you are ready for this?"

"At first, I didn't, "Annie answered truthfully. "I'm too used to doing things on my own strength.

When I started to pray and give my problems over to the Lord, he gave me such peace. I knew that it was time to deal with the past. I know that God is going to give me the strength to get through this."

"That's great! I know this is a big step for you. I'm so proud of you Honey."

"Thanks." Ryan's support meant so much to her.

"And, don't worry," Ryan said tenderly, "we'll take it slow."

"Slow?" Alarm rang through Annie's voice. Was he referring to the relationship or the book? What relationship? Panic began to flow through her. We don't have a relationship! She was in an all out war with herself.

"Annie, don't let those old ghosts come back and haunt you. God wants to heal you, Honey. Don't worry. I promise we'll take this book slow."

"Book!" Annie blurted out loudly. "Good. The book…"

Ryan laughed softly. He felt as though he already knew Annie so well. He could picture her back in Boston getting all panicked. "Annie," Ryan asked gently, "what did you think I meant?"

"The book, of course," Annie tried to sound sure of herself.

Ryan laughed so loudly that Annie had to hold the phone away from her ear for a minute. "Yeah, right."

Annie was about to object but a nervous laugh rumbled out of her instead.

"Sweetheart, we will take this book slow, and, our relationship. I promise I won't ever rush you into anything."

"Relationship?" Annie's tone was startled. "You mean our friendship, don't you?"

Ryan laughed again. "OK," he was obviously amused, "our friendship, if that's what you want to call it."

"Yes," Annie sounded emphatic, "our friendship. We are good friends."

Ryan's voice took on a gentle but serious tone. ""Is that all we are, Annie? Just good friends?"

"We are good friends."

"Nothing more?"

There was a long silence on the other end and for a moment Ryan wondered if she had hung up on him. "You still there?" he asked curiously.

"Yes," Annie replied wearily. "I'm still here but I don't think I can answer your question right now."

"You don't have to. If we're both seeking God's will, then He will lead us."

"True."

"OK, then," Ryan sounded more energetic, "you want to study up on chapter one and we'll discuss it in a few days?"

"That sounds good," Annie was beginning to relax again.

They both said good night and Ryan promised to call Annie in a few days. Long after she had hung up the phone, she sat quietly replaying their conversation over and over in her mind. Annie could definitely feel God healing her heart and she thanked him for it. She knew the road out of the dark, black pit was going to be long and hard, but she also knew the journey out of it would heal her. To experience true healing she knew she'd have to experience and deal with deep pain.

"Thank you, Father," she prayed earnestly, "thank you so much for helping me crawl out of this awful hole I've been living in. Thank you so much for bringing Ryan Jones along. Lord, he's just the type of friend I need. Father, please guide us both as to where this relationship should go. I'm afraid, God, and I really need your help.

Fourteen

"*So*, what did you think of question four?" Ryan asked in a thoughtful voice as he fiddled with the devotional book in his hand.

Annie remained quiet just long enough for him to know exactly what she thought of question four. Ryan laughed loudly into the phone. "Annie, I know you better than you think I do. I knew the first time that you saw question four, you'd hate it." He laughed again and waited patiently for her response.

"It's a stupid question," Annie's anger boiled over into her voice.

"Annie," Ryan's voice was instantly filled with compassion, "sometimes to get out of the valley, we have to go down the mountain even further before we're able to change direction and head back up. We have to go through a harder time for a while before things get better. That's what I believe you're doing now."

Annie grumbled heatedly into the phone. "Sometimes I really get steamed at this author. He makes it seem like, if you go methodically through all his steps, everything in your life will be hunky dory. Well, what if you go through all his steps faithfully and your life still stinks. What if your life isn't coming together like the textbook says it should? Tell me, how many people's lives come together in textbook fashion anyways? Not many that I know of." Annie's voice tightened. "For example, question four! 'Describe to a close friend how you felt when your spouse passed away.' What a completely stupid, idiotic question. How on earth does he think I felt? This whole book is completely annoying, insulting and incredibly dense. I really think that we're wasting our time here."

Ryan laughed quietly. He had anticipated her reaction. "OK, I'll go first."

"What do you mean?" A trace of fear and panic quickly rose in Annie's voice. If he went first did he think that she could go second?

"I'll try to describe to you how I felt when Kay died."

"Uh, Ryan," Annie stuttered nervously, "I don't think that I can do the same for you. I mean," she added agitatedly, "at least not right now."

"That's OK, Annie," Ryan reassured her, "whenever you're ready." He paused for a moment asking God for help. He had dreaded this conversation. This was the hardest subject in his life to talk about. Every time he got into it, he felt like he was living through the nightmare of Kay's death again. It tore him up inside like nothing else could do. Ryan sighed deeply and again asked God for help and then pushed on. "Uh Annie," his voice was filled with pain, "the only other person outside of my family that has heard this story is my pastor." He sighed loudly. "I'm not sure I'll be able to make it through, but I'll give it my best shot."

"Ryan," Annie urged sympathetically, "do whatever is comfortable for you."

"Annie, if I only did what was comfortable for me, I'd never talk about Kay's death at all. It's not an easy thing for me to discuss." He blew out a loud breath. "I don't think it ever will be."

"That's true." Annie understood all too well.

Ryan forced himself to push on. "I guess I should start with how I met Kay. I don't think we ever really got into it except to say that we met at college."

Annie was holding the phone so tightly that her hand hurt. She didn't want to miss a word of what Ryan was saying. It was as important for him to tell the story as it was for her to hear it.

"Kay transferred into Messiah College my junior year." Ryan's voice started to lighten as it took on a reminiscing tone. These were the beginning of the good years for Ryan and Kay. "I was immediately smitten," Ryan admitted lovingly, "and after a few failed attempts, Kay finally agreed to go out with me. She was a shy person, kind of like your Ryan but together we made a great team. We were married two weeks after graduation. After our honeymoon, Kay did secretarial work while I tried to get my music career off the ground. It was very frustrating at times. In those early days, I had so many doors slammed in my face. The industry wanted me to sing traditional hymn like songs and not the contemporary Christian music that I knew God had called me to sing. I mean it, Annie," Ryan said adamantly, "if it weren't for the Lord's strong leading and Kay's confidence and support in me, I never would have been able to pursue this. You know," he sighed frustrated, "there's only so much rejection that a person can take before it buries them alive. At the end of a long day of banging on music executive's doors in Nashville, and all of them basically telling me that my stuff would never sell...there's no market for it and so on, I would get so totally down. So often I felt like the life was being drained right out of me. It was a strange thing," Ryan added reflectively, "I clearly heard the Lord's voice directing me into this field but no one else in the music industry did." Ryan laughed at the irony of it. "No one else but Kay. She was very encouraging and wouldn't let me quit. That girl really believed in me. It's an awesome feeling to know that someone really believes in you. Not everyone has that benefit and even though I only had one person believing in me, I know she believed in me with all her heart. It was one of the best gifts she ever could have given me. It helped me to push on. I know I never would have the music ministry I do today if it weren't for God and Kay's steadfast love and support."

"She sounds like a wonderful person." This was the most that Ryan had ever talked about Kay. Annie wanted to get to know her well because she was such an important part of Ryan's past and an important part of their future together.

"So, how long was it before you got your first contract?"

"Four long years." Ryan closed his eyes as the memory brought back the endless, frustrating journey. "Four long years of trying to sell my music to the industry and four long years of continually being turned down." Annie could hear the pain in Ryan's voice. "It was a very difficult time in my life. I felt a lot of stress and pressure and looking back, it was not the best way to start a marriage. Kay worked long hours to support us and the guilt I felt about the situation was tremendous." Ryan paused. "While I was knocking on doors, trying to get a foot in the industry, I took any job I could to help out. I played background on several other people's demos and albums. They loved my piano playing but weren't interested in my songs. Sometimes I would get invited to audition for an executive at one of the smaller labels. I would go in all excited and sing my heart out only to be told time and time again that my stuff would never sell. There was no market for it." Ryan sighed loudly. "Those were what we called the dark years. God carried us through, and believe it or not, Kay and I just grew closer and closer. We also grew very close to God during this time. We relied on Him like we never had before. We trusted Him, walking a path of faith that I never thought I would be able to walk. The dark years helped build a strong foundation with my relationship with God and my relationship with Kay. Every time the world would knock us down, God was always there to pick us up and carry us on. It was like experiencing the best and worst of life all at the same time. What a roller coaster that was. I think one reason that God allowed us to go through those dark years was that we had to totally rely on Him and completely trust in Him."

"Man, I never realized that you and Kay went through so much. You are a man with an incredible talent. I just assumed things rocketed for you right from the beginning."

Ryan laughed. "Most people have no idea what artists go through before they get their big break. All the long hours, the discouragement, and all the dead- end roads get hard to handle year after year. To push on in a determined way can be very hard when you don't see the light at the end of the tunnel. I can't tell you how many times I wanted to throw the towel in and quit. The idea of a regular 9-5 job sounded wonderful. That would have been the easy thing for me to do but oftentimes what God calls us to do is not the easy thing. That's why I couldn't quit. This was something that God had called me to do. It wasn't about me, it was all about Him. I love the Lord with all my heart and want to please Him and serve Him. How can I ever quit something that I know in my heart that God has called me to do?" Ryan sighed. "I just couldn't. I remember thinking back at the beginning of my career, that I wasn't sure what was going to come first, my big break, or my big breakdown. God knew just how much I could take and oftentimes I felt that He brought me right to the limit on this one. The battle was tougher than any I had ever fought." Ryan sighed loudly. "I have to say, that I have never felt closer to God than when I am in the thick of battle and I know that He is holding me up."

Ryan paused for a long time. Annie began to wonder if he was even still there. "Are you there?" she asked quietly.

Ryan laughed. "Yeah, I'm still here. I was just traveling down a bit of memory lane. The funny thing about memory lane is that sometimes the road is smooth and you fly down it like you're on a super highway. That's a time in life when you feel like everything is going your way. Other times, the road is an old gravel road. You down shift your car and proceed cautiously. You're hitting a few bumps in life, but you feel like it's nothing you can't handle. Then," Ryan laughed loudly, "you hit those times in life when you discover that you're on a dirt road filled with potholes and landmines. Everything seems to be hitting the fan and you're not sure why. You take cover because you don't know what's going to fly your way next. This is a road that you need to go down very slowly and maneuver carefully or you'll never make it through. This is a time in your life that you need to cling closer to the Lord. I mean stick to Him like Crazy Glue. I have looked back at this point in my life many times and have continually come to the same conclusion. This was not a road that I walked down and expertly maneuvered by myself. It was a road that God carried me down and I didn't even know it at the time. He brought me through the minefields and set my feet back on the gravel road. It's an awesome feeling to be carried in the arms of God. It's something that I'll never forget."

"Wow, that is so incredible. I never knew that you went through such a battle."

"It wasn't something that we ever advertised. We always wanted the Lord to be at the center of our lives and not our problems. Besides, "Ryan laughed lightly, "whenever people know that you have problems, you tend to get truckloads of advice. And," he laughed again, "it tends to be a lot of ungodly advice. I honestly understand where these good-hearted people are coming from. It's just that God's ways are so different from the world's way. His ways don't even make sense to Christians sometimes unless they are following Him very closely. Even then," a quiet laugh rumbled out of Ryan, "His ways don't always make sense to me. One thing that I've learned over the years is that God's ways don't have to make sense to me. I'm not called to make sense of His ways; God just calls me to follow them. I've found that our view of the world and situations that surround us change drastically if we have our focus on God. It's as though we're looking at the world through His eyes and not our own."

"That is definitely true."

"Anyways," Ryan continued on, "Kay and I did most of our confiding in each other, God, and a prayerfully selected group of friends. We kept the circle small in order to keep our focus clear. We wanted our eyes on God and not the problems. When you put your eyes on your problems, you'll sink for sure. If you put your eyes on God, He has a way of bringing your focus above your problems and helping you take in the bigger picture of things. He did this for us time and time again."

"I really understand what you're saying," Annie replied thoughtfully. "God has done the same thing for me again and again." Annie paused and then asked anxiously, "What happened next?"

"Well, one day I'm walking around downtown Nashville. I was feeling completely discouraged, and ready more than ever to quit. Four years…"his voice could not conceal his hopelessness. "Anyway, I was walking around Nashville and I see this guy painting a house. It was a very small house and he was working fast. As I stared at him from across the road, he must have felt that someone was watching him because he suddenly turned around. When he spotted me, he waved. After a moment, he asked me if I wanted to join him for an iced tea. I did, and we went into the small house together. The place was so small that you could almost touch the back door and the front door at the same time!" Ryan laughed. "It was an overgrown doghouse!" He laughed again. "So, this guy's name was Clint Copeland and as we began to talk, we soon discovered that we were both Christians! Almost immediately, there was such a bond between us. He was like a brother. We just clicked. As we continued talking, he told me he was fixing up the house to be used as a contemporary Christian recording studio. Well, I was in so much shock that the iced tea that I had just swallowed went down the wrong pipe in my throat." Ryan laughed loudly. "I spent the next few minutes choking, sputtering and gagging like a drowning man. I'm sure it was quite a sight!"

"I can imagine!" Annie laughed.

"After I got over my initial shock, I was able to share with Clint what God was calling me to do. He asked me for a demo tape and the very next morning he called me back. And," Ryan said dramatically, "the rest is history!"

"That's an incredible story!"

"Yeah, but it's not the end." Ryan had grown suddenly quiet. "Are you up for hearing more, or have I worn you out?"

"Ryan," Annie said compassionately, "as long as you're up to talking, I'm up to listening."

"Thanks," Ryan whispered. "Well, the next sixteen years were pretty wonderful. Kay and I felt like we were living an incredible dream. She was able to stop working and stay home with me. Shortly after that, Beth was born and a year later Nikki. Three years after Nikki, David came along. I never knew such contentment and happiness in my entire life. I had a wonderful wife, who I was crazy about, and who was crazy about me, and three beautiful kids. Our life was centered on God, family, friends, and ministry. It was an awesome time."

"Uh, Annie," Ryan hesitated, "here comes the hard part. Are you ready for it?"

Annie cringed inwardly, dreading the moment. She had come to love Ryan and knew that anything that hurt him would hurt her as well. She prayed that God would give her the wisdom and strength to help Ryan. "Yes Ryan," Annie answered as confidently as she could, "I am ready to hear whatever it is that you want to share."

"Well," Ryan laughed nervously, "I am not so sure that I'm ready to share this, so please bear with me."

"Take your time."

"Thanks. It was about six years ago that Kay was diagnosed with breast cancer. It came as an awful, unbelievable shock to all of us. I felt like I had been thrown into a full-fledged nightmare. It was as though we were suddenly thrown down a wild raging river, in a canoe full of holes, without any paddles." He paused for a minute as his troubled sigh filled Annie's ear. Annie was struggling with her own emotions. So many times, after her husband's death, she had felt exactly the same way that Ryan was describing right now. It was the worst feeling that she had ever known.

"I had never felt more helpless in my entire life," Ryan continued quietly. The frustration was mounting in his voice with every word. "I had always prided myself on taking care of Kay and protecting her against all harm. That's what a good man does for his woman. But now," Ryan's voice had gone from frustration to anger, "there was absolutely nothing I could do. For the first time in my life there was nothing I could do and it was almost killing me."

"I'm so sorry."

"Thanks," Ryan whispered. "Oh, I forgot to tell you something. I want to make sure that I don't miss anything. Kay was awful at going to the doctors. She had a fear of them and never went except to have babies or if she was deathly sick from something like pneumonia." He paused again and Annie could feel his deep struggle to go on. She wasn't sure what to say, but then Ryan continued.

"If she had gone to the doctor for regular breast exams," Ryan was choking on his own tears, "she'd probably still be alive today. You know," he said slowly, "talking about the death of a loved one has to be one of the most painful things you can do. The death of a spouse, one you had a great marriage with and loved with all your heart hurts so deeply that I find it difficult to describe or talk about. It," Ryan paused thoughtfully, "it's simply numbing."

"I know exactly what you're saying, Ryan," Annie was fighting hard to control the emotions in her own voice. "When you're at the alter and the two of you become one, it's a union so strong for some that death can not break it. I have often felt, as the surviving spouse, like I've been cut in half. Ryan was such a huge part of me that the hole left in my heart feels like a cold, empty, desolate spot. I feel like something will be forever missing without him."

Ryan cleared his throat. "I know what you're saying, Annie. I get angry when I think about Kay's death. I get even angrier when I feel that it was probably something that could have been prevented." Ryan sighed loudly. "I guess I just feel cheated. We have both been cheated out of 'happily ever after'."

"I agree with that. Forever is not supposed to come until you're at least 100. Actually," Annie paused thoughtfully, "I don't think that anyone in a happy marriage wants forever to arrive. Even if they both have a long, happy life together, forever would still arrive too soon."

"But, we will see them in heaven again," Ryan spoke gently. "It's important to keep an eternal perspective on this."

"I know. I hold that in my heart. But," the anger was growing in Annie's voice again, "life continues to go on, regardless of situations and personal devastations. I remember standing outside the busy city hospital in Boston and staring in disbelief that life just went on. Doctors and visitors were going in and out of the hospital, a man on the corner was selling flowers and balloons, another guy across from him was selling hot dogs." Annie sighed. "I wanted to scream at the top of my lungs. I wanted to make them all stop and tell them that someone so special had just died. I wanted them to care about Ryan's death like I did." Annie choked back a sob. "Instead, the hot dog man kept selling hot dogs, the balloon man sold flowers and balloons, and the doctors and visitors continued flowing in and out of the hospital doors. Life just went on."

"Life never stops for everyone," Ryan said gently, "it only stops for those who are hurting. It's cruel that way."

Annie agreed. "I don't think I'll ever stop missing Ryan or wishing he could be around to watch the kids grow up. I wish so much that he were here to share in the kids lives. To be a part of their accomplishments, acknowledgements, and achievements, and then be there to support them and love them through their defeats. It's hard to try to be both mom and dad."

"I hear you. I have thought the same thing a thousand times myself. Little everyday things remind me of Kay. I miss the smell of her perfume,

I miss the way she would triple knot her sneakers so they wouldn't come untied, I miss her smile, her warmth, her laughter, and most of all I miss her love. I loved the way she loved me."

"Ryan," Annie struggled for control of her wobbly voice, "I miss so many of the same things." Annie paused to wipe her tears on her shirtsleeve. "I don't know when I'm ever going to be able to stand in our kitchen and not think of Ryan. Remember how I said he was making his famous spaghetti sauce when he died?"

"Yes."

"Well, I haven't been able to cook sauce in my kitchen since he died. It brings the whole incident back in my face full force." Annie sighed heavily. "It was a year before I could even go down the aisle at the grocery store that holds the sauces and pastas. It was too painful."

"Sometimes, everything reminds you of the one you loved and lost."

"That's true. I used to resent people who told me that I should just get over Ryan's death. I later came to realize that there was no way for them to understand my pain because none of them had lost a spouse." Annie took a deep breath. "Do you honestly think that it's ever possible to really get over the death of someone you loved so much?"

"I feel like eventually you accept the situation forced on you because you have no choice. You learn to deal with the reality of it, but no, I don't think you ever get over it. I don't think you ever get over losing someone who has impacted your life so richly and that you have loved and been loved by so freely."

"I agree. Now, what about the pain? Does the pain ever go away so that when you think of them, it's just great memories and not great memories laced with pain?"

Ryan exhaled loudly. "I think that time lessens the pain, some anyway, but from my experience, there will always be a certain amount of pain because the loss is so great and you miss them so much."

"You know," Annie said softly, "it's a strange thing how love and pain go hand in hand. No one else can cause you deeper pain than those you love. Yet, on the flip side of that, no one can bring you greater joy than those you love."

"That's true," Ryan wiped away some tears. This was a hard discussion to have but he knew it was one that he and Annie needed to have. He was glad she had opened up so much.

"Well, to finish my story," Ryan pushed himself on before he knew he wouldn't be able to, "the first year after Kay's death was awful. I hurt so badly that I wanted to die. I stayed pretty reclusive. I didn't tour at all. I stayed home trying to hold my hurting family together. We were all in such pain, but God had his hand on the Jones family. He held us together and bonded us closer through all the tearful talk and late night chats. We opened up to each other like we had never before. And we prayed...we prayed like we never had before too. You pray differently when you're at the bottom of the bucket and hurting so much that you want to die. You don't hesitate to level with God and cry out for help." Ryan sighed. "Slowly, somewhere after the year point, we began to heal. After two years, the pain and hurt lessened. They have not gone away completely, and to be honest with you, I don't expect them to. We will always miss Kay and love her but we can't dwell on her not being here. My family had to make a conscious choice to move on. We will never forget her, but if we don't move on, we'll never survive either. It's important to go on living. You have to go on with your life."

"Yes," Annie agreed quietly, "it is important to move on."

"So," Ryan asked in a lighter tone, "are you ready to tell me why question four was such a dumb question?"

"Well," Annie laughed sheepishly, "I think I'd like to retract my earlier statement. It is a good idea to talk to a trusted friend. I've just never been very good at discussing private hurtful issues with anyone."

"You're doing fine with me."

"Yeah, but you've been through the same thing I have. And," Annie added thoughtfully, "you're easy to talk to."

"Thank you." Ryan sounded smug.

"I mean it. I have a tough time opening up. Things are different with you."

"I know what you mean," his voice was sincere this time, "thank you."

"You know one thing that still bothers me?" Annie was growing angry again. "I know that God could have prevented Ryan and Kay's deaths. He's God," Annie stated as if that explained everything. "He can do anything. I really believe that. So, tell me why he didn't choose to heal two people who really loved Him and lived a Christ-like life? I just don't get it. I don't think I ever will."

There was a brief silence that was broken by Ryan exhaling loudly. "That's a tough one, Annie. I've thought of that many times and questioned God about it a lot." He paused. "Annie, I don't think you're going to like the answer that I'm going to give you."

"Try me."

"Well, after a year of throwing that question in God's face, I finally realized that I wouldn't heal if I didn't let go of my anger. And," Ryan sighed, "that included my anger aimed at God. I was so mad at Him. I felt the same way you did. I knew that God could have healed Kay but for some reason, He chose not to. I finally had to accept the fact that God's ways do not make sense to us all the time. I had to take this issue on faith. God knows the bigger picture. He has his reasons and if I didn't leave it in His hands, I was going to go crazy."

There was a moment of silence before Annie spoke. Her words shot out angrily like they were fired out of a noisy gun. "You were right. I didn't like your answer one bit!"

Ryan smiled. "I knew that you wouldn't. You're still holding onto your anger against God. To understand where I'm coming from, you have to ask God to help you let go of your anger. It's the only way to get on with your life."

"You know," Annie replied heatedly, "I know in my head that you're right. It's my heart that I'm still having trouble with. My heart is still very angry at God."

"I know, Annie," Ryan whispered lovingly. "I'm praying for your heart. I know that God will heal your heart like He did mine but you've got to let Him. He won't force His ways on you, you've got to let Him, Annie."

"I hope you're right," Annie whispered.

"I'm never wrong," Ryan answered confidently.

Annie burst out laughing. "Oh, really?"

"Kidding, I'm just kidding! But," Ryan added seriously, "God is God. He can do anything and that includes healing you and me."

Fifteen

On November 18, Annie drove down to the Coast Guard Station in New London, Connecticut, to meet Tyler's ship. She hadn't seen him in three months and she missed her son terribly.

On the way back to Boston, Annie and Tyler talked non-stop, catching each other up on all the latest news. Tyler's cruise had been a relatively uneventful one this time. Annie always worried about Ty when he was out to sea for extended periods of time. She knew he could face all sorts of dangers in the form of storms, boredom, loneliness, and the temptations those can bring, along with loose women in every port. Ty was a strong Christian young man, but his good looks, along with his charismatic personality made him a target for the girls. Even though he was firm with unwanted advances, Annie still worried about him. She had to. She was his mother.

"So," Tyler narrowed his eyes at his mom for a minute, "tell me about Ryan Jones. You mentioned him a lot in your letters, but," he stared at her intently, "I'd really rather hear the stories from you personally."

Annie knew that Tyler was going to have a problem with her friendship with Ryan Jones. Even when her husband was alive, Tyler was always very protective of his mother and little sister. His 6'9" athletic frame could be very intimidating if he wanted it to be, and, being in the Coast Guard had taught Tyler how to handle himself even better. He was not only her son, but also her self-appointed bodyguard.

After his dad's death, Tyler became even more protective of his mom. He saw the pain she was going through first-hand, as many nights Annie cried herself numb in Tyler's loving arms. When men would come, and invite Annie out for an evening, she didn't have to deal with turning them down. Tyler always did before she had to and she was grateful for this.

"Mom," Tyler's voice reflected the impatience that was building within him, "are you going to talk to me?"

Annie stopped reminiscing and smiled at Tyler lovingly. "Ty, you're going to like him when you meet him someday."

"Listen, mom, I'm worried about you. I don't want some guy, even if he is a famous Christian singer, playing with your heartstrings."

"That's why you have to meet him, Ty. I know you're going to like him."

"Don't be so sure about it." Tyler sighed. "It sounds to me as if you've already made your mind up about him."

Annie was quiet for a moment. She didn't like the accusing tone in Ty's voice, but she knew he was concerned. "Tyler, I'm not sure what to say here." She glanced over at her son quickly. "I know I'm serious about being his friend...but I can't commit to anything more than friendship at this time." Annie glanced at her son. "He knows that."

"Good," Ty replied firmly. He didn't like this one bit. He didn't want any man hurting his mom.

Two days later, Annie and Tyler flew off to Chicago to attend the Christian Writer's Awards Banquet. Annie was so nervous about the whole thing. Going up in front of people was not her thing and the thought of having to go up on stage in any capacity frightened her. She was a behind the scenes type girl, not a stage person. She prayed that God would keep her calm and help her survive the night.

The night of the banquet, Annie and Tyler arrived at the auditorium dressed to kill. Annie wore a beautiful, traditionally styled long black gown and Tyler wore a black tux. She thought her son looked so handsome. She couldn't help but smile as she sneaked proud motherly glances at him.

During the dinner, Annie felt too nervous to eat. Tyler came to the rescue, gladly devouring her chicken dinner. "After the dinner," Annie coached herself, as she went over the schedule in her mind, "we go to the awards ceremony, and then to the ball." Annie couldn't wait to get to the ball. It wasn't that she was such a great dancer, in fact she didn't even know how to dance. She just knew that by the time she got to the ball, it would mean that the award's ceremony was over, and that would be a wonderful load off her mind.

As Annie and Tyler took their assigned seats in the large auditorium, Annie prayed earnestly to God. "Please God, don't let me win. I'd probably get so nervous that I'd pass out, and if I didn't pass out, I'd trip on my gown, or get so tongue tied that I wouldn't be able to speak. Please, please help me."

Annie tried hard to force herself to relax as the different categories were awarded. They had already done, "Historical Fiction", "Mystery/Adventure", "Westerns" and now "Sci-Fi" was being presented. "Romance" was up next, which was her category, and she was so nervous that she was shaking like a leaf. This did little to help boost her confidence. It was difficult to convince yourself that you were going to do fine when your body was trembling like you were going through an earth-quake.

When the presenter came out on stage, Annie broke out into a cold sweat. Tyler put his hand tenderly on his mother's arm. She tried to smile at him but she couldn't. She felt like she was going to throw up, pass out, or maybe do both.

"Oh why," Annie thought as the panic swelled inside her, "why did they have to put me in the first row? There's no place to hide!"

As Annie forced her mind to focus on the presenter, her eyebrow rose questioningly as she listened to him. He wasn't mentioning any of the writers up for the award. Instead, he was talking about a special presenter for the award. Annie relaxed a bit as she gratefully realized she had a little more time.

Just then, in an enthusiastic voice, the presenter announced, "I'd like you to give a big warm welcome to our special presenter, contemporary Christian singer, Mr. Ryan Jones!"

Annie stared up on stage thinking she had only imagined the presenter saying that. Her doubts quickly evaporated as Ryan strolled onto the stage and the audience exploded with cheering. She stared at Ryan in shock, as she felt a thick fog numbly encompass her brain. Her mouth swung open in surprise and she quickly put a hand over it because at the moment she felt incapable of closing the gaping hole.

She knew she should try to act casual and cool, but she couldn't. It was hard to act laid back when you felt as though you couldn't breathe, think, or move. All she could do was stare up at the handsome man on stage like some sort of brainless idiot.

Tyler eyed his mom heatedly and then leaned over and angrily whispered in her ear. "Did you know that he was going to be here?"

Annie shook her head slowly, as she took in Ryan's stunning appearance. He looked absolutely gorgeous in his black tux, with it's long tails, and his crisp white shirt. As he reached the podium and flashed his famous charming smile, Annie was quite sure at that point that she had never seen anyone more handsome in her life. He took her breath away, threw her off balance and left her reeling for control. Though her reaction to him still surprised her some, she was becoming more used to it, and even half expecting it. This seemed to be the standard reaction she had to him every time she saw him. There was just something about the man that moved her deeply.

As she continued to study Ryan, she was struck by his apparent ease before an audience. He talked easily with them as though they were a group of old friends. Annie tried to listen to him, but between her shock at seeing him, and her panic of being at the awards ceremony, she couldn't focus on much of anything.

Ryan's gaze found her and held her eyes with his own in a tender embrace. He smiled at her so lovingly that she felt that her heart and mind stopped working. Time stood still. Everything just stopped. For a brief second, it was as if the two of them were the only ones in the room. With a look, he managed to calm her fears some, and set her heart at ease.

When Ryan ended his introduction, the audience rose to their feet clapping enthusiastically. Annie stiffly rose from her chair, feeling awkward and completely lacking any of the social graces that she might have possessed before. Panic washed over her like a tidal wave as she tried to recall whose name Ryan had announced. She couldn't think of it to save her life. What if it was hers? She'd look stupid staying by her seat when she should be up on stage. But then," Annie thought on the verge of going crazy, "if it's another author's award, she'd look even more stupid going up on stage. At that precise moment, she wanted to die. Nervously, she glanced around the audience to see if anyone was heading up toward the stage. No one was, and this was making matters worse. Everyone was looking at her, smiling, clapping, and cheering.

"Go on, Mom," Tyler urged.

Annie looked up on stage and saw Ryan looking down at her with an odd mixture of pride and amusement written across his face. When she made no move to go, he impishly wiggled his pointer finger at her, indicating for her to come up on stage.

Annie's feet felt stuck in cement. She looked up at Ryan and felt completely horrified. In a flash, Ryan went down the stage steps, and over to Annie's front row seat. He lovingly offered his arm to her, and when she took it, he carefully escorted her up on stage. Ryan led her to the podium and slowly let go of her arm. He stood a few feet off to the side of her, watching over her protectively.

After Annie gave her acceptance speech, which came off with amazing ease and sincerity, Ryan approached the podium, and handed Annie her award statue. He winked at her, and then gave her a professional, congratulatory hug. Then, offering his arm again, in a gentlemanly type way, he escorted her back to her seat. As she sat down, he quickly leaned over and told her he would see her at the ball. Then he rapidly walked up the center aisle and left the auditorium.

As Annie sat back in her chair, she wondered for a second if it had all been a dream. She looked down at the award in her lap, and it confirmed to her baffled, completely confused mind that it had all really happened. As her body started to relax, a thought struck her hard. She couldn't believe that Ryan had come all the way from Tennessee to Chicago to present the award to her. His kindness made her eyes well up. She knew he was slowly working his way deeper and deeper into her heart.

As Annie and Tyler exited the auditorium, Tyler kept glaring at his mom with a serious expression tightly masked across his face. In an angry voice, his words tumbled out. "Mom, I wasn't expecting to see him tonight."

"Tyler," Annie addressed her son firmly, in a clear warning tone, like only a mother can, "give him a chance. If you honestly don't like him once you've gotten to know him, then I'll respect that. But right now, tonight, I want you to give him a fair chance. Do you understand me?"

Tyler slowly nodded his head and reluctantly agreed to his mother's request. As they entered the ballroom, with a waltz in progress, Tyler leaned down to speak to his mom. In a voice that sounded remarkably like a bratty two year old, he demanded the first dance. Annie nodded, and Tyler took his mom in his arms and swept her onto the dance floor. As they moved around the dance floor, Annie couldn't help but keep an anxious eye out for Ryan.

When the song ended, Annie and Tyler made their way to the side of the ballroom. Ryan appeared a moment later, followed by his three children. The girls were both in elegant black gowns, and David wore a tux that matched his father's, complete with long tails.

"You guys!" Annie bubbled over excitedly and she quickly hugged Ryan and his kids, "I can't believe you're here! I'm so surprised!"

They all laughed and then David told her how his dad had planned the trip right after they got back from Boston.

"And you never spilled the beans." Annie smiled coyly at Ryan. He grinned proudly back at her.

"Oh!" Annie suddenly grabbed Tyler's arm and pulled him up next to her. "This is my son, Tyler." Annie made the rounds of introductions and the four of them greeted Tyler in such a warm, loving way that he found he couldn't help but smile right back at them.

Nicole was studying Tyler intently and he looked down and uncomfortably met her gaze. She went over to him and looped her arm through his. "You know handsome," her tone was playful and teasing, "it's a good thing that you're my cousin. If you weren't, I can guarantee that Beth and I would be fighting over you like cats and dogs."

Everyone laughed, and then Nicole led Tyler to the dance floor. Her 5'4" frame dwarfed against his

6'9" height. "Man, you are a tall one!" Nikki had tilted her head back to look up at him.

Ty laughed as a wide grin spread across his face. "Yeah? Well you're puny! You must not have eaten your veggies as a kid! Ever hear of Wheaties?"

Nikki laughed. "Yeah, the Breakfast of Champions!"

"Well maybe you should try some."

Nikki laughed again. "I go for the cereals that have good toy prizes. I've got quite a collection of cereal toys at home."

Ty laughed. "You're probably still eating Happy Meals, too."

"Hey, don't knock Happy Meals. I love Happy Meals! They have really great toy prizes!"

"You're something else."

"Thank you."

"It wasn't a compliment," Ty teased.

"I'll take it how I want to, and I'm taking it as a compliment."

They both laughed. Nikki waved her finger at Ty and he leaned down a little. "Tyler, don't tell anyone here tonight that Beth and I are your cousins. We want to make the other girls painfully jealous!"

Ty stood up straight again and laughed loudly. He liked his new cousin and her spunky spirit. He winked at her and joked, "Hey, I'd do anything for family!" They laughed some more and soon began talking like old friends. Some of Tyler's reservations about Ryan Jones and his family started to melt away.

A few yards from where Tyler and Nikki danced, David was awkwardly dancing with his sister Beth. Annie and Ryan, who were on the sidelines, watched the kids as they talked. "I'm so glad that Nicole jumped on Ty from the beginning. Her infectious smile and energy will help him fit right in."

Ryan nodded and smiled. "Yeah, that's Nikki. She's a real ticket. She's always had a gift for making people feel comfortable."

Ryan then walked in front of Annie and bowed slightly. "My good Lady, would you give me the pleasure of this dance?"

"Oh Ryan," Annie was instantly anxious, "I really don't know how to dance."

Just then, a fellow writer came over and asked Annie to dance. In a smooth move, she grabbed Ryan's hand and led him onto the dance floor. "I'm sorry Clay," she said over her shoulder, "I've already been asked for this dance."

As Ryan took Annie in his arms, and gracefully began to waltz her around the dance floor, he eyed her suspiciously, "What's the deal? I thought you just said that you didn't want to dance? Are you only dancing with me because you don't want to dance with Clay?"

Annie giggled. "I'm dancing with you, Mr. Jones, because I want to dance with you and not Clay!"

"So you really want to dance with me?"

Annie was surprised by the hint of doubt that she heard in his voice. "Of course I want to dance with you!" She squeezed the hand she was holding. "I know that you have quite a reputation for being an incredible dancer. I can't dance and didn't want to embarrass you or anything."

"Embarrass me!" Ryan sounded astonished. "Are you kidding? Here I am dancing with the most beautiful girl at the ball. How could I ever feel embarrassed?"

Annie smiled and thanked him. "I've missed you."

Ryan's eyes glowed. "You have?"

Annie nodded shyly.

"Well Darling, I miss you all the time!" Ryan swung her in a circle. Annie laughed and Ryan winked at her.

"Hey, thanks for saving me at the awards ceremony." Annie was sincerely grateful. "I was completely panic stricken."

"I could tell," Ryan's voice was soft and concerned. "I'm glad I could be the one to present you with such a special award. I'm so proud of you Annie. Your work has touched so many lives."

"Thank you." Annie was tearing up. "So has your work. Your music has made such a difference in so many lives around the world."

"We're all simply vessels being used by God. That's the important thing," Ryan paused thoughtfully, "that our lives glorify God."

Annie nodded and as they continued to dance, Ryan gently laid her head against his chest. Softly, he whispered loving words to her. "It's so good to have you with me again Annie. I love you and being separated from you is pure torture."

Annie shyly looked up into Ryan's blue eyes. She could see in his eyes a reflection of what she felt in her own heart. Once again, Annie got the feeling that she would melt from all the love she saw in his eyes. Annie smiled up at him lovingly as she thanked God for bringing such a special man into her life. She knew he was a keeper. Ryan Jones knew how to show a woman the softer side of love, and, he did it extremely well. He'd send her flowers and cards, small gifts and mementos, but nothing could equal the tender way he treated her, as if she were the most precious treasure on earth. His tender, gentle unconditional love, won her over, time and time again. Annie didn't think there was a woman alive who wouldn't fold under this kind of treatment. It was love at its purist.

Annie began to notice the curious glances they were receiving from people around them and then the reason for it hit her. "Ryan," her tone was urgent, "we've danced three dances straight. People are staring at us. Maybe we should change partners for a while."

A serious expression spread over Ryan's face. "Annie, I have never cared what 'people' in general have thought." His voice was firm and filled with his usual confidence. "I am out to please God, family and close friends alone. I don't ever want peer pressure to make my decisions for me. I want to do what's right in God's eyes regardless of what anyone thinks." He studied Annie carefully for a moment before going on. "As for changing partners, I strongly object. I want to dance every dance with you and hold you for as long as I can." He flashed a charming smile at her. "Any objections to that?"

Annie shook her head slowly. "How can there be when you put it like that!"

"Good." Ryan pulled her a little tighter. "I wish this night would last forever."

Annie agreed and slowly laid her head back against his chest. She felt as though she were walking on a cloud. The ball flew by so quickly that

Annie felt it had almost been a dream. It was magical. It was one very wonderful, incredible dream that she knew she would replay again and again in her mind.

Around 11:30, the party began to break up. Ryan gathered the group around him and suggested an idea to them. "Why don't you and Tyler come to the airport with the kids and me? Our plane doesn't leave until three and it will give us all some more time together."

Everyone excitedly agreed and the six of them crammed into a cab for the ten minute ride to the airport. When they got to the airline terminal, they dropped themselves down in an empty corner and continued their conversation.

"Hey, Beth," Ryan looked over at his oldest daughter, "do you have those pictures that I asked you to bring?"

Beth rummaged through her pocketbook until she produced an envelope holding twenty-four pictures in it. "Dad asked me to take these pictures of the ranch for you guys so you could see what it looks like."

"Yeah," Nikki added mischievously, "we want you to know what to look forward to when you come down at Christmastime."

"Mom?" Tyler asked confused. "Christmas?"

"Ty," Annie tried not to sound too excited, "we've all been invited to Chatfield Hollow for Christmas. What do you think?"

"Tennessee? Christmas?" Tyler's tired mind was trying to make sense of it all. "What about Uncle Bob, Aunt Jude and Heidi? Aren't they expecting us to come down to Boston for Christmas?"

"Yes, Ty," Annie nodded, "but the Jones family has invited them too. Wouldn't that be great!" Annie couldn't contain her enthusiasm any longer. She thought Christmas in Chatfield Hollow would be perfect.

"Mom," Ty's voice held concern, "things are tough at Uncle Bob's job right now. There's no way he's going to be able to spring for airfare from Maine to Tennessee."

Ryan jumped in before Annie could answer. "Tyler, they won't have to pay airfare. It's included in the invitation."

Tyler and Annie stared at Ryan in shock. Beth and Nicole couldn't help but laugh at their expressions. "You're kidding?" Annie mumbled out.

Ryan shook his head. "Think of it as my Christmas present to you."

"Ryan," Annie immediately protested, "that's way too much. I wouldn't feel right about accepting it."

Ryan laughed. "OK, Annie, think of it as my Christmas present to myself. I want all my east coast family with us this Christmas." Ryan paused and looked at Annie intently. "The kids and I have prayed about this a long time before we acted on it. We feel this is the right thing to do. Besides," Ryan winked at her, "you've got to come. I've already paid for the tickets."

"You have the tickets?" Annie shouted at him.

Ryan nodded and smiled at her again. He didn't hide the fact that he found Annie quite amusing. "Yeah, we were planning to Fed Ex the tickets to you next week." Annie stared at Ryan with an expression on her face that was hard for him to read. "Annie," Ryan was exasperated, "we're so glad that the Lord has brought you into our lives. Family means so much to us. It's such a special treasure. Is it so bad that we want to spend Christmas with ya'll?"

Annie shook her head. "No, it isn't."

"OK, then," Ryan moved to sit next to Annie, "let us take care of the tickets. God has blessed me with the means. Please don't embarrass me."

Annie leaned over and hugged Ryan. "Thank you," she whispered. "That's very generous of you."

"Yeah," Ryan teased, grinning at her, "it is, isn't it?" Annie rolled her eyes at him and smacked him playfully on the arm.

Ryan turned to Tyler. "How do you feel about this?"

Tyler looked over at his uncle and studied him for a second. "OK," he answered thoughtfully. "I think it would be nice to spend Christmas with all of you." A loud cheer went up from the group and Annie got up and hugged her son tightly.

"Ty," Ryan asked in a serious voice, "there's something else, isn't there?"

Tyler looked at him and nodded slightly. "You know," he sighed loudly, "I was very determined not to like you."

"It's a natural feeling," Ryan said easily.

Ty nodded again. "I was so close to my dad, that I couldn't even imagine another father figure in my life. I didn't want one." Ryan nodding understandingly. "My mom wrote letters...lots of them," Ty looked at his mom lovingly. "She filled me in on everything. I knew you and dad were twins and that you looked a lot alike. But," Ty slowly shook his head, "nothing could prepare me for the moment I saw you up on stage tonight. I couldn't believe the resemblance." Tyler sighed again. "For a brief moment, I thought I was looking at my dad."

"I know exactly what you mean about the resemblance thing." Ryan smiled at Ty. "When your mom showed me the picture of your dad, back at the concert hall in Rhode Island, I felt like someone had knocked the wind right out of me. I was completely floored. I knew it was the brother that I had been searching for." Ryan looked directly into Tyler's eyes. "I just knew it."

Tyler nodded. "I tried hard to convince myself," he went on in a small voice, "that I couldn't like you because you looked so much like my dad. I thought if I liked you, I wasn't being loyal to my dad."

Ryan nodded understandingly. His eyes clouded with tears and he bit his lower lip for a minute. "Ty," Ryan's voice was choked up, "I think I really understand what you're saying. But," he leaned forward with his elbows balanced on his knees, "I think that the more you get to know me, the more you'll see there are plenty of differences in our personalities. That should help you separate the two of us some."

Ty smiled. "Yeah," his own eyes had clouded over, "that's true. I already see differences. You're more outgoing than my dad was. Even though dad was very friendly, he struggled with shyness all his life. I don't think you have a shy bone in your body!" Everyone laughed.

"Hey, ya know, I do occasionally have shy times." Ryan tried to sound defensive and everyone just laughed harder.

"So," Ryan eyed Ty with amusement, "have you noticed any other differences?"

"Well," Ty grinned like a wise guy, "you are a few inches shorter than my dad. You must have been the runt!"

The laughter rang out again. Ryan pretended to act insulted but the group just laughed harder. "I'm 6'2" you know, and for your information, that is not exactly a runt."

As the group laughed, Ryan asked Tyler if he noticed any other differences. "Don't worry about hurting my feelings," Ryan said sarcastically, "I can take it. Us runts are really pretty tough, ya know."

Tyler laughed at his uncle. As he ran a hand through his short Coast Guard buzz cut, he added thoughtfully, "You're more persistent than my dad, more of a poet, and more romantic."

"Romantic?" Ryan asked curiously. "How can you tell?"

"My family has listened to your music for years. The love songs you write," Ty suddenly felt embarrassed and directed his attention to his feet, "well, they're pretty incredible. Somehow God gives you the words to express your heart like no one I've ever known. It's a gift."

"Thank you, Ty," Ryan studied the floor for a minute. When he looked back up at Tyler, his friendly, loving expression had vanished. A hard, serious, heated expression now covered Ty's face. "What?" Ryan felt confused.

"I'm not quite sure how to put this." Tyler was looking at Ryan intently.

"Just spill it out."

"Well, you're good with words and pretty good looking...I just don't want you hurting my mom." Tyler's words hung heavy in the air. As he maintained eye contact with Ryan, he grumbled, "If you ever hurt my mom, I'll throw you off a boat in the middle of the ocean and watch the sharks chew on you. Do you understand?"

"Yes. That's quite an interesting picture you've put in my head," Ryan eyed Tyler intently. "Now I think you should hear my side of the story, from me." Ty nodded. "I promise you, right now, that I will do my best to never hurt your mom. Did your mom tell you that I only dated three woman in my entire life?"

"Really?" Tyler was completely shocked.

"Yes, and one of those girls I married. Dating was something that I never did lightly."

"Really?" Ty sounded just as surprised as he did before.

Ryan sighed deeply. "Why does that surprise everyone so much?"

Tyler laughed. "Probably because your rich, good looking, a celebrity and extremely outgoing."

"I'm not a playboy, Tyler." Ryan had grown frustrated. "I never have been. All those qualities you just mentioned aren't the ones that are important. What matters most is what's in someone's heart."

Tyler agreed. "That's true." He looked at Ryan a moment before continuing. "Since we're talking so openly here, do you mind if I ask something?"

Ryan smiled. "Not at all. Shoot away."

"OK," Tyler stared at Ryan like a hunter focusing in on his target, "what exactly are your intentions with my mom?"

The room grew very quite. Ryan held Tyler's gaze a moment before answering. "Ty," Ryan's face broke into a huge smile, "your mom has informed me that we are just friends. She says a close friendship is all she can handle right now."

Tyler nodded, and then glanced over at his mom as an amused expression grew on his face. "Just friends, huh?" He wiggled his eyebrows at her. It was obvious he didn't buy that for a second.

Ryan continued quietly. "Now I'm going to tell you the other side of it. Everyone else here knows it. I agreed to take our relationship slow because that is what she wants. It's what she needs right now. But," Ryan grinned broadly, "I will also tell you that my steps, slow as they may be, are walking toward forever with your mom. I don't want you to have any doubts about that. I am walking toward forever with your mom." Ryan repeated himself and then paused thoughtfully and smiled again. "I am head over heels, totally in love with your mom." Ryan looked at Tyler intently. "Does that answer your question?"

Tyler laughed. "You left no room for doubt."

"Good. I wanted to be perfectly clear."

"You were crystal clear." Tyler laughed. "It was all how I thought it was but I needed to hear it from you."

"Are my feelings that obvious?"

"Are you kidding?" Tyler grinned. "It's written all over your face. And," Ty added quietly, "the way you treat my mom, well, it wasn't very hard to figure out."

Ryan nodded. He looked at Annie, who had remained very quite throughout the conversation. Ryan gently took her hand and placed it firmly in his. "Are you alright, Honey?" Annie nodded. "Good," Ryan added humorously, "because I wanted to make sure that you weren't going to pass out on me again." Everyone laughed and Ryan gave Annie's shoulders a quick squeeze.

"Yeah," Tyler smirked, "I heard about that."

"How?" Annie demanded.

"I have my sources." Ty winked at his mom. When Annie continued to stare, he gave in. "Amy," he said in a matter of fact tone, "she wrote me a very interesting letter."

"Wait until I get my hands on her," Annie muttered. Once again, everyone laughed.

As the room quieted down, Ryan suddenly got serious. "Ty," he said with urgency in his voice, "there is something else that you should know too. Your mom is sorting through a lot of things right now. She made me promise that our friendship would go slowly. I never want to push her in any way. I intend to honor that request, even though at times it's like a slow, torturous death, killing me by the inch." Ryan laughed. There was more truth to that statement than he cared to admit. "I want to give her the time she needs."

As he lovingly squeezed Annie's hand, she looked tenderly into his eyes and thanked him. He winked at her playfully. "Annie," he smiled at her, "I have to play by your rules. You're holding all the cards." Annie smiled back at him.

"Hey," Ryan squeezed her hand again, "do you want to go for a walk with me?" Annie nodded and they slowly began making their way around the airport.

"I want you to know," Ryan began slowly, "that I meant every word I said to Tyler."

Annie smiled at him. "I know. You're always being so good to me. You are kind, thoughtful and sensitive." She laughed. "You don't play fair." Ryan smiled lovingly. "You treat me so nice that it makes it difficult for me to ever say no."

Ryan's eyes darkened. "Then don't, Annie. Don't say no."

Tears started running down her cheeks. "Ryan, you know I can't say yes, at least not right now."

Ryan nodded knowingly. "I'm prepared to wait, Annie. I've already told you that. I'm not pressuring you, but also," his voice grew heavy and pained, "I don't want to be competing with a dead man. The memories, the years…I can't do it. I won't do it." He sounded adamant. "You need to be able to take me as I am. I would do anything for you Annie. I love you with all my heart. But," he grabbed her arm to stop her from walking, and looked directly into her eyes, "you need to take me as I am. I want you to love me for who I am. I can't ever be Ryan Smith. I can only be me and I need you to really understand that."

"I do understand that."

"Good," he said strongly, "because when you say yes to my proposal, I want you to be saying yes to me and not him. Do you understand what I'm saying? It has to be just the two of us. If it's a trio, it will never work."

"Ryan," Annie said resolutely, "I would never do that to you. That is why I'm asking you for more time. I want to make sure that everything in my heart is straightened out. You need to be the only man in my heart. I know that. Please, give me a little more time, and, keep praying."

Ryan nodded and hugged Annie tightly. "I just needed for you to understand where I was coming from."

"I do."

Ryan's expression melted as his face broke into a huge smile. "Now those are words I'm hoping to hear from you very soon, Honey. Are you practicing there Annie, getting ready for the real thing?"

Annie smiled and tugged on his hand to lead him back to where the kids were waiting. "You're funny."

"Annie," Ryan grinned at her charmingly, "I'm not trying to be funny. I really look forward to hearing those words from you."

Annie couldn't look at Ryan. She knew if she did, she'd burst into tears. She was honestly sorry for what she was putting him through but she knew she couldn't commit to him until she was sure he was the only one in her heart.

All too soon it was time for the Jones family to board their plane back to Chatfield Hollow. Annie hugged each of the kids tightly and then turned tearfully toward Ryan. "I hate good-byes."

Ryan nodded as his own eyes filled up quickly. He pulled her into his arms and held her in a cherished embrace, as though he never wanted to let her go. He quickly brushed a kiss across her check. As he eased away from her, while he was still holding her hands gently, he spoke to her in a voice that was so tight he could barely get out the words. "I love you, Annie. Never forget it, and never doubt it."

With his eyes he held her a moment longer. She could see the passion, the longing and the desire burning in his eyes. There was a hunger between them. She knew that her eyes mirrored the same heated emotions. It was an aching of the heart, which was worse than physical pain, that two people who were in love had to endure when they were apart. The air sizzled between them with a fire she knew would never die out. They had something very special. Annie knew that most people didn't get to experience this kind of love even once in a lifetime. Here God was granting it to her twice. As she hugged Ryan good–bye again, and watched him disappear to his plane, she felt as though he were taking her heart with him. She wondered how long it would be until she was ready to fully accept his love. She prayed to God it would be soon.

Tyler put a loving arm around her as they walked from the airport. Silence surrounded them both as they were lost in their own thoughts and in their own worlds. Both of them had a lot to think about and a lot to deal with. So much had happened in the last few months. There was no turning back now. It was only straight ahead. Yet, Annie thought, biting her lip and holding back the tears, her straight ahead had a few more valleys in it that she knew she'd have to go through. Valleys were never easy, but she knew it was necessary to go through them to end up on the mountaintop. It was the only way, and she knew it was a way that she could only face with God at her side.

Chatfield Hollow

A New England Novel

Sharon Snow Sirois

Available Winter 2003
at
Your Local Bookstore

Chatfield Hollow

Chatfield Hollow is the exciting conclusion to Stony Brook Farm. This fast-paced romantic comedy bounces back and forth between Massachusetts and Tennessee almost as quick as the teasing and joking do between Annie and Ryan. They both enjoy surprising each other in their own unique and creative ways.

As the chemistry between Annie and Ryan intensifies, they slowly begin to take their relationship in the direction of forever. Not everyone is happy with their decision, and they are faced with obstacles that could tear them apart.

Through the battles, Annie and Ryan grow closer to the Lord and closer to each other. Annie learns to stand up and face her accusers instead of running away. She comes to realize that Ryan Jones is not only a man worth fighting for, he is a man that she is head over heels in love with and doesn't want to live without.

One

$\mathscr{C}$hristmastime, and all it's splendor had finally arrived and Annie and her family excitedly boarded an airplane bound for Chatfield Hollow, Tennessee. Annie's older brother Bob, her sister-in-law Jude, and her five-year-old niece Heidi drove down from Maine to Annie's Stony Brook Farm so they could all fly out together. Little Heidi was so excited about her first plane ride that she had already talked nonstop across four states. Annie kindly volunteered to put Heidi next to her for a while so her parents could have a break from the energized chatterbox.

After ten minutes of listening to Heidi yak, Annie knew she was going to have to come up with an alternative plan to quiet the motor-mouth down for a while. "Heidi," Annie firmly addressed the young girl, "I'll make a deal with you." The five-year-old loved making deals and her ears immediately perked up. "How would you like to have this yummy lollipop?"

The little girl nodded her head so vigorously that Annie was afraid she'd get whiplash. "Oh yes, Auntie! I want the lollipop!"

"OK," Annie unwrapped the grape pop, "there's one condition." Heidi looked anxiously at Annie. The little girl loved candy and her face clearly displayed the message that she would do anything for the pop. "If you take the pop," Annie waved it in front of her, "you've got to promise to keep it in your mouth."

"I can do that!" Heidi squealed.

As she eagerly accepted the candy from her aunt, muffled laughs went up from behind Annie's seat. Annie leaned around her seat slightly, and spoke to her children in a voice that was full of warning. "Knock it off you two."

Tyler and Amy looked like they were going to explode in laughter. "Mom," Ty leaned forward and whispered, "I can't believe that Heidi's falling for that old trick!"

"Shhhh," Annie commanded. "Don't ruin it or I'll put the chatterbox next to you." The amusement drained from Ty's face immediately and he suddenly became very serious. "Besides," Annie grinned mischievously, "you guys always fell for it, why wouldn't Heidi?"

Annie turned her attention back to Heidi. She looked like she was enjoying the pop but had a puzzled expression on her face. "What's wrong, Honey?" Heidi garbled a response to her aunt that Annie couldn't understand because the pop was still in her mouth.

"Sweetie, take the pop out of your mouth for a minute so Auntie can understand what you're saying."

The little girl shook her head emphatically no. She didn't want to take any chances of Annie taking her pop away. Her determined blue eyes stared up at Annie again and in a louder voice, she slurred out the word, "Sorree."

Annie studied the girl for a moment feeling more confused then ever. "Sorry? Sweetie, what do you have to be sorry for?"

Heidi shook her curly blonde head again, and in an even louder voice, with more determination, she screamed out, "SORREE!"

This was not going according to plan for Annie. Instead of Heidi talking nonstop, she was now shouting out slurred sounds. They had no connections to any words that Annie recognized; yet the assumption for Heidi was clear. If she yelled these sounds louder at her slightly dense aunt, she might get the message. It suddenly struck Annie that Heidi was playing the same game but with new rules.

"Mom," Amy sounded amused, "I think that Heidi wants you to tell her a story." Heidi confirmed this by jumping excitedly in her seat as loud giggles escaped her slurpy mouth.

"Oh," Annie responded less than enthusiastically, "Do you want Auntie to tell you a story?"

Heidi nodded excitedly. She tucked the pop firmly in the right side of her cheek, and loudly whispered, "Bout the ranch."

"You want to know about the place we're going to?" Once again, a firm nod from Heidi confirmed this was true. Annie inwardly groaned. She had figured out a way to keep Heidi quiet for a while, but Annie knew there would be no peace and quiet if Heidi succeeded turning her into the story-time fairy.

Annie looked at her niece. "Heidi, I'll tell you a short story and then we're both going to be quiet." Heidi nodded her head a little reluctantly and then Annie, even more reluctantly, started talking about the ranch.

Annie went on to describe the horses, the wagons, the sleighs, the barns, the fields and the mountains. She described what each of Ryan's children looked like, and told a little about their personalities. When she had finished, Heidi gazed up at her anxiously.

"What?" Annie asked in a low grumble.

Heidi looked nervously at the pop stick in her mouth and Annie gently pulled it out of her mouth. "What is it, Honey?"

"What does Mr. Jones look like?"

"He's tall," Annie handed the pop back to Heidi, "and he has brown hair."

"What color are his eyes?" Heidi studied her aunt intently before putting the pop back into her mouth.

"His eyes are blue."

Heidi pulled the pop back out of her mouth. "Do they twinkle like mine? Mommy says my blue eyes twinkle."

Annie laughed. "I guess they do." She felt a bit embarrassed discussing Ryan's twinkling eyes with a five year old. It was time to end the conversation, before her inquiring mind went into its investigative reporting mode. "OK, Heidi, I want you to rest some now. We're going to be there soon." Heidi stuck the pop back in her mouth and to Annie's amazement, she was quiet the rest of the trip.

Ryan, Beth, Nicole and David excitedly met the passengers when their plane landed in Nashville, Tennessee. Ryan immediately scooped Annie into his welcoming arms and hugged her tightly. Annie hugged him back just as tight.

"I've missed you so much!" Ryan looked at her so tenderly that she got the feeling she would melt in a puddle right at his feet.

"I've missed you, too! We're all so glad to be here."

Ryan winked at her and then went to greet the rest of the family. Amy and Tyler gave Ryan big bear hugs and Bob and Jude shook Ryan's hand firmly. Bob held Ryan's hand a moment longer than necessary. Ryan knew, in that brief time, a fifteen second inspection was being done by Annie's very protective older brother.

"I look forward to getting to know you." Bob's voice was firm and his manner extremely serious. He definitely wasn't friendly; then again, he wasn't al- together outright frightening either. It was a place somewhere in the middle that wasn't intended to be comfortable for Ryan. It was at that point that Ryan knew, without a doubt, that he was going to be interrogated by Bob. He could see it in his eyes. He didn't care that Ryan was a celebrity, rich or had fans circling the globe. What his eyes plainly told Ryan was that all he cared about was his interest in his little sister.

Ryan smiled as the big man released his hand. Bob's attitude toward him actually made Ryan respect him more. He knew that if he ever had a sister, he'd react the same way. Bob was Annie's self-appointed bodyguard. He was caring and kind, but noticeably protective, defensive and clearly warning those around her that he wouldn't hesitate to permanently maim or destroy, if necessary. It was all in a day's work for Bob and part of doing the brother job.

As Ryan glanced around, he spotted Heidi. He went over to her and knelt down next to her to see her. "Welcome to Tennessee, Little Lady." Ryan offered her his hand and she shook it seriously. Heidi stared at Ryan so intently that he finally asked her if something was wrong.

"You have blue eyes," she stated in a matter-of-fact way.

Ryan's eyes lit and a huge grin spread across his face. "Yes," his voice was amused, "I do have blue eyes and," he tweaked the tip of her nose playfully, "so do you!"

Heidi nodded seriously. "Auntie says that you have twinkling blue eyes."

Ryan picked the five-year-old up in his arms and stood up. His laugh could be heard throughout the terminal. He glanced at Annie impishly and then turned back to Heidi. "Oh yeah, Short Stuff, what else does your Auntie say about me?"

Heidi instantly knew that she was part of a game. She let a loud stream of giggles flood the air. Before she could answer any more of Ryan's probing questions, Annie gently scooped Heidi out of Ryan's arms. She didn't want Heidi giving him the five-year-old version on anything else that pertained to her. Kids definitely had a way of bringing an entire new level of humility to adults.

"Come with Auntie, dear. Let me show you where you get your suitcases." Heidi took off with Annie toward the baggage, looking curiously back at the group. Everyone behind them let out a loud laugh and slowly followed the fleeting pair.

As Ryan caught up with Annie and wrapped a loose arm around her shoulders, Jude discreetly took Heidi's hand and pulled her back with the rest of the group. "Why don't you want me talking to Heidi? She seems very informative." The grin on Ryan's face told Annie that she going to get teased.

"She's too informative for a five-year-old."

"Information's good," Ryan was grinning wickedly.

Annie cleared her throat. "Yes, well, at times it can be but I'd like to make two points here. Information is good as long as it's not about me and if it's coming from your five-year-old source, it's likely to be watered down a bit."

Ryan laughed loudly. "Yeah, well I may have to take whatever info I can gather on you because I remember you telling me that you didn't like to talk about yourself. You're a very private person."

Annie smiled. "You can ask me whatever you want. If you go to Heidi for info on me first, I'll clobber you."

Ryan stopped walking a second and stared at Annie. "I thought you didn't want to answer my questions. I distinctly remember you saying that your life was none of my business."

Annie laughed. "Did I say that?"

"You did, and you know it."

"Listen, you can ask me anything. I've become a very open person."

Ryan's eyes narrowed. "Oh, really? Then the first question I'm going to ask you is why the sudden change of heart?"

Annie laughed. "Because…Heidi is staying in your house for the next two weeks and she's a nonstop talker."

Ryan howled with laughter. "Gee, if I knew that would have worked, I would have invited Heidi down to the ranch months ago!"

"Very funny!"

"I'm serious."

Annie's eyes narrowed. "You'd better not be."

"Are you threatening me?" Ryan laughed. "Remember, I have a talkative five-year-old in my house and I know how to make her talk. I'm very good at opening kids up. Kid's like me."

"That's because you're a big kid yourself."

"Thank you."

Annie sighed. "Promise you'll come to me first?"

Ryan grinned. "This is a very interesting situation here."

"No, it's not."

"You're getting nervous about what Heidi might say."

Annie sighed again. "Yes, I am. If you only knew all the stuff she's blabbed about Bob and Jude. I mean, the kid answers questions honestly and is entirely too informative. She has absolutely no discretion at all. I can't tell you how embarrassing it is at times. There are things I now know about Bob and Jude, because of Heidi's big mouth, that I definitely didn't want to know. She's really awful. You should watch what you say around her."

Ryan laughed. "You see, I wasn't planning on saying a whole lot around her. I was just planning on doing a lot of listening. You know, there so much you can learn about people if you just sit back and listen."

"I think this was a bad idea."

"I think this was a very good idea."

"You're a pest."

"That's nothing new to you. Actually," Ryan laughed, "I believe you called me a pest shortly after we met."

"That's because you are."

"I'm so glad that you're all here." Annie laughed. "I just bet you are–especially Heidi!"

Ryan laughed. "Yeah, I bet I'm going to learn all kinds of things about you."

"About everyone else, too. She never stops talking."

"I'm mainly interested in what she's going to say about you."

"I'm sure you are."

Ryan grew serious. "Annie, I'm sure everything is going to be fine. Don't worry."

"That easy for you to say. You don't know Heidi."

"She's a kid."

"She's lethal."

"I'm sure we'll all have a great time."

"I think I'd have a better time if Heidi got laryngitis for the next two weeks."

"I don't think anything can stop her."

"You're probably right."

"Hey, now, we've been through this before. I," Ryan pointed a finger at himself, "am always right."

Annie laughed, but her mind was still on Heidi. It's amazing how much damage the little rug rat could cause with her loose lips. It wasn't that Annie had anything awful to hide; it was just that Heidi had a way of revealing life's most embarrassing moments that you definitely didn't want revealed. There was a line on how much someone could be humiliated in front of others before permanent damage took place. Annie knew she'd have to leave it in God's hands. As she prayed, she tossed the idea of laryngitis up to her Heavenly Father. It really did seem to her that it would help the situation all the way around.

About the Author

Sharon Snow Sirois, a former teacher,
has been writing stories all her life. She
and her husband have been active in youth
ministry for over twenty years. Sharon is
an avid reader, who enjoys hiking, sailing,
biking and skiing. She is a home schooling
mom who lives in Connecticut with her
husband and four children.

Sharon loves to hear from her
readers. You can write her through
Lighthouse Publishing or email
her at: sharonsnowsirois
@hotmail.com